POWDER

Railers Legacy
Book 3

RJ SCOTT

V.L. LOCEY

Love Lane Books

Copyright

Powder

Two weeks. No promises. Just passion... until the Winter Games change everything.

Jack O'Leary, veteran defenseman and captain of the Railers, isn't sure where his life's headed. Fresh off a painful divorce and staring down the end of his career, he books a vacation to clear his head—romance not included. But when he meets a fiery young snowboarder who refuses to let him hide behind his walls, Jack finds himself falling hard for the first time in years. When their paths cross again at the Winter Games, Jack must decide if he's brave enough to chase the future he never expected.

Tian-Lei Cai-Wilder's living the dream—endorsements, medals, and the bright spotlight of snowboarding fame. His reward? Two weeks in the sun to finally breathe. Meeting Jack wasn't part of the plan, but the gruff, gorgeous hockey legend is impossible to resist. Their vacation fling burns hot and ends clean… or so Tian thinks. When they're both chosen for Team USA, sparks fly all over again—only this time, the whole world is watching.

Powder is a steamy age-gap, opposites-attract, second-chance sports romance featuring a brooding hockey veteran, a golden-boy snowboarder, and a fling that refuses to stay in the past.

Dedication

To my family who accepts me and all my foibles and quirks. Even the plastic banana in my holster.
VL Locey

Always for my family.
RJ Scott

RAILERS LEGACY

POWDER

RJ SCOTT
& V.L. LOCEY

Love Lane Books

ONE

Jack

"NOT TO BE UNKIND, BUT IS THIS *REALLY* ALL YOUR stuff?" I stared around the last two boxes of hockey memorabilia at my sister, Fiona. She was the prettiest thing, and no, that wasn't me being biased because I'm her older brother. Long strawberry blonde hair, bright blue eyes, slim and fit, and the owner of two dimples that flashed when she smiled. I nodded as I put the boxes of old sweaters, milestone pucks, and skates as old as Fiona onto the kitchen counter. "Christ, Jack, that's fucking depressing."

Oh, and she was also brutally honesty, but thank the saints she'd learned to curb that, or her job as a private flight attendant would have ended on day one.

"I wanted Paula to be well-settled," I mumbled, knowing full well my darling sister would come unglued over that comment.

"'Settled' is one thing. Giving her the house, the cars, the dog, and everything else she demanded is another."

I'd heard this all before. A hundred times. Maybe five hundred. And while I loved that my sibling was on the defensive about me even though she was a hundred pounds lighter and eight inches shorter than me, she was known to get in a person's face to stick up for me. My ex-wife Paula was one of the biggest examples. Fiona and Paula had never gotten along. The divorce had not improved that strained relationship. Fiona called my ex a horse and my ex called Fiona an ogre. The two of them fought way more than Paula and I did throughout our marriage. You have to care to fight, and Paula didn't care how it turned out.

"Fi, please, I'm not in the mood," I said then sighed as I looked around my brand-new bachelor pad. One bedroom, one bath, a spacious but empty living room, a kitchen, and a tiny laundry room. All very nice, quite expensive, and overlooking the Walnut Street Bridge, a famed bridge that'd been closed in the seventies but was now used by pedestrians and bikers for access to City Island. It was home now. Not exactly the sprawling three-bedroom, two-bath, two thousand two hundred-square-foot with a two-car garage I'd bought for Paula after our wedding ten years ago in Elizabethtown. I mean… not even close. But it was mine. Empty. Which was kind of how my chest felt whenever I thought about how I'd failed my wife.

"Do keep in mind that she did cheat on you so that should have earned her nothing over the fifty-fifty split the state says she was owed," Fiona fired back as she shimmied up to sit on the smooth white counter, her long red/gold ponytail sliding over her shoulder. A nice summer breeze blew in through the window over the sink. May was already warming up nicely. "Not sure why you felt that she deserved so much in the settlement when all she did was sit around, and sleep with her yoga instructor."

I rolled my eyes. "For the last time she wouldn't have gone looking for another man if I'd been home more," I repeated clearly and slowly in the hopes she would absorb it.

She reached out to flick my forehead. With a porcelain nail painted soft pink. It stung. "Jonathon Patrick Killian O'Leary, you've taken too many hits to the head if you really believe that. Loads of spouses are faithful when their men or women are on the road. She was just using that as a reason to do a double down dog split up the ass with Sage Happy Hatha for three years while you were out bleeding all over the ice."

"I rarely bleed all over the ice, Fiona Katherine Margaret Shillelagh O'Leary. I make other men bleed all over the ice."

She flicked my brow again. "Do not add that walking stick moniker to my name. The three plus the surname are bad enough." I snickered. "And it will not dissuade me from talking about the nag who now owns your dog and drives your cars."

God, she was tenacious. "The dog was hers, a gift, and the car was also hers. I have my truck. I don't need or want a pink Audi. How would it look for the captain of the Railers to pull up to the barn in a bright pink car with fake eyelashes over the headlights?"

"Seriously, why does she have to be such a real-life Barbie?"

I didn't have an answer for that. Paula had been a few years younger than me, yes, and so stunningly beautiful that I'd never quite felt fit to be with a young woman of such incredible beauty. She'd modeled in New York before we got married. I'd never found her fondness for pink or her affinity for tiny purse dogs odd. She'd been bubbly and fawned over me. For the first few years. Then it all started to go wrong. I was away too much, she was lonely, life wasn't as glamorous as she'd expected, and on it went.

"You're too nice."

I shrugged. Yeah, maybe so, but when I loved someone, I showered them with affection. That was how men were supposed to act around their heart's desires. Our father had spoiled our mother terribly. Forty years of wedded bliss they'd had before they'd lost their lives to a drunk driver one dark winter night back home in Montpelier. God, I missed them. They would have been heartbroken and so disappointed in me for allowing my career to ruin my—

"Ow, fucking hell, stop doing that," I snapped after another hard flick to my forehead. "I'm going to dunk you in the Schuylkill if you do that again."

Fiona gave me a soft push on the chest. She knew I was full of hot air. I'd throw myself into the river that flowed through Harrisburg before I chucked her in it. Now, when we were kids…

"Okay, I'll drop it. For now. Do you want me to call a designer to come in and add some life to this place? It has nice bones, Jack, it just needs some color and maybe a picture on the wall that isn't of a hockey rink?" I leaned my ass on the counter. The place was sparse, but I really didn't care about all that silliness. "Right, I see that pucker on your forehead so what I'm going to do is make sure you have things like drapes, a nice bedding set, as you left all the sheets and towels in the house for your horse of an ex—"

"*Fiona…*"

She flipped her ponytail, then winked. "Sorry, it's her teeth."

"Her teeth are fine." They should be. I'd spent tens of thousands of dollars on them. Not that she had modeled again once we'd gotten married, but she liked to be pretty. I liked to look at pretty women, and some men on occasion, and I had the cash, so why not give her what she wanted?

Fiona waved a dismissive hand. "I'll outfit the place for you because I love you and know that if I don't get you set up properly, you'll be drying yourself on paper towels after a shower."

You do that one time in college, and your sister never forgets.

"I also wanted to talk to you about taking a vacation." I must have made a noise as she tsked me instantly. "No, no, do not make that Dad sound. He always did that when he disliked something. Sucked air between his teeth. You need to get out into the world, Jack, meet new people, maybe have a wild affair."

"Nope, I… no, I do *not* want to have a wild affair with anyone." I walked out of the kitchen to the living room, folded my arms, and planted my feet. This was my captain's stance. Next, I locked my jaw. My captain's expression. Men of great size and meaty fists would see me like this and not push.

Fiona, on the other hand…

"Honey," she cooed as she followed me into the cavernous room. I really did need a couch to soak up the sound. "I'm not saying you have to propose to anyone. Please, don't. But just get your willie wet with some bouncy beach babe or surfer dude. Flush that rancid memory of Trigger from your mind and heart." She came around in front of me, tipped her head back, and met my glower with a loving look before snuggling close for a hug. I kept my arms crossed for about a millisecond before opening them and embracing her. She smelled like vanilla and a flowery scent. "I want you to be happy again. You've been so sad since the divorce decree. I know it was a letdown for the team to get knocked out in the first round, too, so all of this is sitting on your chest. Let me see if I can find a nice sunny destination for you. Somewhere packed with singles, where you can lounge on a beach, sip drinks with paper umbrellas, and reacquaint yourself with how damned charming and handsome you are."

I tucked her head under my hairy chin. I'd yet to shave my red playoff beard. I tended to cling to things for far too long. My marriage, for example. My beard. My old running shoes. My ten-speed. My skates and sticks from my days at Bowling Green. My ragtag collection of Timmy Horton hockey cards. Several pairs of boxer shorts.

"Not sure I'd say handsome," I mumbled as we hugged it out. My nose was off-center from being broken in a game against Pittsburgh five years ago, then again against the Raptors two years ago. I had surgery scars on my left shoulder, a knee that swelled when the atmospheric pressure dropped, and a jagged white line on my jawline from an errant stick to the kisser that had resulted in ten stitches just this year. Hockey was a tough game.

"See, that right there is your ex talking." She gave my side a pinch then tilted her head up to gaze at me. "You're very handsome. Some would say rugged. Beefy, tough as nails, sweet as a honey roll—"

"Do not say that honey roll crap anywhere near the barn or the Railers locker room. The kids like Gunny and Trick need to know that I'll grind them into paste if they don't play up to their potential."

She smiled up at me. "I think they know that you're a goober belly." She jabbed my gut, which was not goober-bellied at all but nice and tight. I worked out every day. I even had abs under the thick pelt of reddish-blond hair on my belly. "But I'll be sure to extoll your pasting abilities when I see them next."

Which wouldn't be until September. The season was over, our lockers cleared out, our hopes dashed. Sure, we'd made it to the first round, but then we'd tanked. I'd told the press I was sorry for letting the team and the city down. I'd been so into my own personal shit that I'd not given the team my full one hundred percent on the ice. Our failure was on me. I was the captain. It was down to me to talk the guys up, keep the locker room pumped, and ensure the team stayed mentally on track. I'd failed at that. Just like I'd failed to keep my wife happy and—

"Ow!" I winced at the nail flick.

"You had that I-suck-and-want-to-wallow-in-my-suckiness look on your face." She reached up to rub my brow. "Sorry, but you need someone to keep you from sliding into that pit of self-loathing that your ex kicked you into with her infidelity. And since we only have each other now, that person is me."

"I love that you're my pit person," I confessed. She nuzzled in for another hug. "I'll think about a vacation." I couldn't see it as her nose was smushed into my chest, but I knew she was smiling her smug smile of success. "I said I'll think about it. Do *not* make reservations."

A WEEK LATER, I WAS ROLLING MY BOXER SHORTS THAT didn't have elastic showing into tight little logs because Fiona had made reservations and lined up a round-trip flight to Belize. Caye Caulker to be exact. She listened about as well as the Yorkie Paula toted around in oversized bags and called Bapsi-Boodles.

After hurriedly shoving my clothes into my suitcase, I sat on it and shouted at it because I was in a bad mood and couldn't bring myself to yell at Fiona. Deep down, I knew she was only trying to pull me out of my funk. She loved me and thought a couple of weeks on a Caribbean island would help me feel better. Which, sure, it probably would to some extent, but if she thought I was going to go wild and jump into bed with the first man or woman who looked at me, she was very wrong. Yes, it had been over eighteen months since I'd been with someone intimately. My hand didn't count, although even using that had started to decline.

I just wasn't interested. Mom used to say that I loved with my whole being. I guess that was true because ever since Paula and I split, my sex drive has been pretty low. I've never been the type to go for one-night stands. I prefer some emotion, or at least for the person I was with to know my name, as silly as that sounds. I've had two girlfriends, and I married one. In college, I also dated a man for a few months, but the pressure from school and hockey was just too much. Plus, it was much easier to ask out girls. Not that I did that much. That first girlfriend was my steady from junior year through graduation. Then she moved west, and I got drafted by the New York team, where I met Paula. I fell pretty hard.

We'd gotten married, and she had packed up to move several times before we settled in Pennsylvania when the Railers picked me out of the reduced-for-quick-sale bin. Turned out to be the best thing for me, and the Railers, as I thrived on the ice and was named captain in my third year. The move to the Keystone State did not do my marriage any good. Paula was dour by then, complaining steadily about the dullness of this state, how she longed to return to Manhattan, and how I was unable to meet her emotional needs when I was away so much. Obviously, I wasn't satisfying a few other of her needs. And if that wasn't a kick in the balls to a man's ego, I don't know what was.

The alarm on my phone rang out, pulling me from the memories of the past. I latched my suitcase, grabbed the handle, and made my way out of the bedroom to the living room. Over the past week, Fiona had flown to Paris with a wealthy businessman in a private jet and had been tipped five grand for her exemplary service. Seemed she knew how to make a dry martini just the way the rich dude's mistress liked them. Guess no one really cared about vows or fidelity anymore. Anyway, the tip had been blown on my condo. I now had furnishings, plates, pots, a few plants that I would kill sure as hell before the snow flew, and a TV set with a PlayStation. Among all the things delivered here, I used the TV and game console the most. And the bed. The new sheets and duvet were nice; I had to give my sister that.

A text arrived while I was shoving my wallet into my back pocket. Fiona reminded me not to miss my flight, or she would hire a boat to float me to Belize. I hit her back with a kind and loving reply.

I'm 37 yrs old. I know where the airplanes are. – J

I got a row of big eyeballs as a reply. Yeah, yeah, she was always watching me. Shouldn't I be the one keeping an eye on *her?* I was the oldest after all. Not sure how our dynamic had changed so drastically. I made a last check of the condo, patted my ass for a wallet check, stuck my cell into the front pocket of my jeans, and grabbed my suitcase. Down the elevator I went to the lobby to find the ride Fiona had arranged— she wasn't taking any chances that I would not get to the airport—waiting outside the tall tower I now called home. No one waved goodbye, no one kissed my cheek, no one wished me a safe flight at the door.

Being single sucked.

The ride to Harrisburg International was pleasant enough. I'd left my beard on my face, just neatened it a bit, so fans would be thrown off if they spied me at the airport. Not that I didn't love our fans, I did, but man they could be rough. If one more dude bro came up to me to inform me we'd shit the bed last month I just might run out onto the I-83 and be done with it all. My driver was pleasant but not overly chatty. I arrived with two hours until boarding, checked my bag, went to the bathroom, and bought a soda that I downed. I took my time, no rushing, and made my way with ease through the TSA checkpoint. On the other side I found a seat facing the runway, my sight locked on the planes being readied for their flights. I'd flown a lot in my years. I mean a *lot*. I had no idea how many miles a hockey player logs in his life, but it was enormous. I'd flown into snowstorms, thunderheads, and the tip of a hurricane. I'd landed on ice strips where the plane went sideways after landing. Once we were blown off-course on a takeoff from Chicago-O'Hare. One time we lost an engine and had to turn around over the Canadian wilderness.

As my group was called to board I ambled forward, carry-on resting on my shoulder, without a care in the world. While some others around me were chatting nervously, I was plotting out my nap. When you've flown into a flock of birds and lived to tell the tale there was little that was going to make this flight to paradise anything other than mundane. Since Fiona had booked me in first class—on her—I settled into the large seat in the middle with a seat on my right and one across the aisle. I loved it. Seriously, a guy of my size did not do well in coach. Knowing I could stretch out without getting dirty glances from the people in front of me was everything.

The plane filled quickly. I texted Fiona a selfie of me all tucked into my fancy nook. The doors were closed then, and I found myself scanning the cover of the book I'd picked up in the airport when there was a commotion up front. The door was reopened. Glancing up from my phone, I watched as a man hurried onto the plane, his dark hair windblown as if he had raced through the airport. When the guy glanced my way, my stomach dropped. His dark brown gaze locked with mine for a second. He nodded at the flight attendant and then made his way to his seat. On my right. The smell of citrus and sweat curled around me as he rushed to stow his carry-on down by his feet. I stared. I couldn't help it. He was perhaps the handsomest man I'd ever seen.

He flashed me a smile that made that turbulent feeling reappear. I hurried to buckle my belt before I did something stupid like gasp and tumble into the aisle. Team captains didn't gasp at sexy men.

TWO

Tian
_____

"I'M GONNA BLAME THE LIMO," I'D SAID TO NO ONE AT all. "Who knew even a private limo could be late?" I practiced as I skidded the final few steps to the plane.

Being late had *nothing* to do with the fact that I'd spent way too long editing a video in the first-class lounge and had lost track of time.

All the private limo driver's fault.

Obviously.

By the time I'd taken off my headphones and heard the *final call* blasted over the speakers, I had to sprint from the lounge all the way to the gate. My lungs burned, my shirt clung damp to my back, and I practically parkoured over rolling suitcases to get there.

I made it just as they were closing the door, sliding through with a disarming grin that only half-softened the flight attendant's pissy glare. Hot, sweaty, heart racing, I hurried down the aisle—and then froze when I saw where I was sitting. Not because it's first class, because I'd earned this sweet deal, and my sponsors loved me, but because there, in seat 2A, sat the most beautiful thing I'd ever seen. Jack freaking-hard-as-nails O'Leary. Hockey god. Railers captain. Legendary defenseman. And the eternal thorn in the side of my beloved New York team.

I flashed him a smile because, wow, it was Jack O'Leary, in the flesh.

I dropped into the seat to his right, still catching my breath, fumbling the belt until it finally clicked home. The steward hovered nearby, no longer scowling but still making sure every buckle snapped, and every tray locked as if the fate of the flight depended on it. Heat radiated from me, sweat damp at my collar, and I tried to play it cool while sneaking sidelong glances at Jack O'Leary like this was no big deal at all.

The captain's voice crackled over the speakers, the announcement muffled and half-lost in static as usual. I caught something about taxiing to the runway and takeoff being scheduled at oh-something, but the rest blurred. I leaned back, trying to focus on breathing, pretending like I wasn't coming apart with excitement at *Jack O'Leary* sitting right there.

Say something.

"I reckon they take lessons in how to speak over the intercom," I said out loud, and to my shock he glanced at me. I grabbed the chance, cupping my hand like a mic and slipping into my best crackly-static pilot impression. "Good evening, ladies and—krrshhhh—gentlemen, we'll be—krrrshhhh—taking off—krrrshhhh—end of the century—krrshhh—and the weather in wherever the hell we're going is… probably fine." I let the words trail off in more static and static-filled mumbling, grinning sideways to see if he'd bite.

He didn't bite.

He looked kind of shellshocked.

I cleared my throat, wiping my palm on my shirt before extending it toward him. "Tian," I said, trying to sound casual. "Professional snowboarder, occasional idiot who nearly misses flights, and your seatmate, apparently." My grin widened, nerves bubbling under my skin. "Nice to meet you."

"Jack," Jack O'Leary-NHL-Star said.

"Oh, I know!" I blurted before I could stop myself, words tumbling out like an avalanche. "You're the Railers captain—defenseman, all-star, the guy who's been carrying the team since forever. Not the same since the old guard, y'know? The Tennant Stan years, right?" I winced the second it left my mouth. "Oh, wait, I didn't mean it like that. Crap. Verbal diarrhea. Sorry. What I mean is… I'm a New York fan. And you—you're kind of the bane of our existence."

He raised an eyebrow, and I studied his features. I wasn't small… well, I was, kind of. Five-nine, wiry, muscles, sure, but not built like Jack. I'd never grow a beard that could match what he had—nor do I think I ever would—no big loss, since my skin was smooth as a baby's behind because of one of my more lucrative sponsor deals with Heavenly High Cosmetics. They were also the reason I was flying out of Harrisburg instead of my hometown of Denver, after I visited their head office for a recent photoshoot.

His beard looked insanely soft, and his piercing blue eyes showed confusion as he stared at me. A look I knew all too well. I knew I was in people's faces too much; Mom always said my personality was bigger than my body. I couldn't help wondering if Jack was proportionate. Oh fuck—did my gaze just drop to his lap? Shit. Was I checking him out? He'd kill me. I'd be dead in the bathroom with a hockey puck shoved down my throat.

"Sorry," he rumbled, and I blinked at him, my cheeks heating.

"Huh?"

"For being the bane of your team's existence."

"Oh yeah, I—" The plane gave a little shudder as it began to move, slow and steady, to the taxiway. Words tumbled out of me again before I could stop them. "You can't help being one of the best," I said, then rolled my eyes at myself. *Smooth, Tian. Real smooth.* "You deserved better than going out first round for the Cup."

Jack quirked his eyebrow—ginger-blond, unlike his

fully red beard—and the corner of his mouth twitched. "Given it was New York who took us out, I thought you'd be happy."

"Dude," I said, groaning inside even as the words slipped free, "we knocked you out in four games. It was too easy."

Fuck. Why did I say that?

Jack's frown deepened, and he turned his attention back to the book in his hand, shutting me out. My stomach dropped. Great. I'd offended him. My mouth had this way of running ahead before my brain even engaged, and now the silence between us felt sharp enough to cut.

"Shit," I said, and touched his arm so he looked at me. "I didn't mean—"

Jack sighed and spoke, his voice lower now. "You didn't offend me, Tian. It wasn't just you guys. We barely scraped into the playoffs, and we lost because we didn't have enough heart. Left it all on the young guys, and that's on me as captain. New York was strong this year, no question. But we'll get you next year."

Wow. He sounded beaten down, used up, like he was done with it all. And that? That was on me, for running my mouth without thinking. I was overexcited, buzzing on adrenaline and nerves. After all these years, I had solid sponsorship, and this trip to Caye Caulker was my prize from them for being, in snowboard speak, a total powder hound who could throw down clean tricks when it counted. An amazing winning dude. And here I was, ruining it by talking trash to Jack O'Leary.

I couldn't fix it straight away; the engines rumbled louder as we taxied, the plane picking up speed, every bump in the tarmac jolting through me until gravity pressed me back in my seat and the nose lifted. My stomach swooped with takeoff; my words trapped behind clenched teeth as the ground dropped away from us. He read his book through the whole thing, not a care in the world, while I clutched the arms of my very comfortable first-class seat as if it were a lifeline. I'd hurled myself off cornices that made other riders blanch, spun clean off cliffs with the drop yawning beneath me like nothing, just another day on the mountain. But flying? Nah. Flying was different. Flying, I hated. I counted down every damn second until we leveled out.

And then my gaze caught on the gorgeous, built-like-an-outhouse Viking beside me. Jack looked like a bear without any of the soft parts, all bulk and harsh edges, and I couldn't help wondering—what does that make him in gay slang—me being five-nine, slim, wiry, more like an otter than anything? Before I could stop myself, I blurted out, way too loudly, "Our last main season game, you played like thirty-one insane minutes on the ice, two assists, and blocked eleven shots like it was nothing. I remember because I yelled at the TV when you crushed our power play. I'm kind of a fan of yours," I admitted, words rushing out too fast. "Back when you were in New York, I followed you obsessively. Not in a creepy stalker way, not just you, the team, I mean. Peak obsession." He glanced at me and gave me the magic eyebrow, and I sank deep into my seat, convinced I'd just screwed this whole thing up. But then Jack closed the cover on his book.

He studied me for a beat, then said slowly, "You remember all that? Huh." He sounded surprised. "Most people don't care about blocked shots unless it's their guy in front of the crease." His mouth twitched, almost a smile.

The flight attendant rolled up with a tray, offering drinks and fancy displays of snacks—no tiny bags of pretzels in first class, clearly. I took the plate of snacks —tiny ramekins with warm mixed nuts, olives, and neat little squares of cheese, plus a couple of fancy crackers —stuck to water because my mouth was dry from running and nerves, and Jack asked for coffee, black. I considered how long we'd be partners side by side on the flight—Harrisburg to Belize was, what, about five hours in the air? Plenty of time to dig myself in deeper, or maybe, just maybe, make him laugh once before we landed.

We chatted for the longest time, right through a delivery of salmon with asparagus and a tiny ramekin of truffle mashed potatoes, the kind of fancy first-class plating that made me feel out of my depth. The ramekin was like a child's toy in Jack's hands, and I couldn't stop watching him. He held tight to his book that he'd read none of.

"You like books?" I fished for something to say.

He tilted the cover just enough for me to see—some thriller by an author I hadn't heard of. "Don't get to read much," he said. "Bought it in the airport. Figured it might help me get in the holiday mood."

"By reading a murder mystery?" I teased.

His mouth quirked, and God, his smile was gorgeous. His eyes were gorgeous. For a second, I forgot how to breathe.

"Who knows what's gonna happen in Belize," he mused.

I grinned at him. "Maybe someone gets offed with a toothbrush. Airport purchase gone wrong. Classic whodunit."

"A toothbrush."

"Yep. No one suspects the old lady in the raincoat, wielding a toothbrush."

"In a raincoat? On a tropical island beach."

I leaned in conspiratorially and ran with it. "Picture it—sun blazing, palm trees swaying, and there's this sweet little grandma in her plastic raincoat, trudging along the sand. Everyone thinks she's harmless, just another tourist who packed wrong. But secretly? She's a cold-blooded killer. Toothbrush sharpened to a lethal point, minty fresh death on the beach. CSI: Caye Caulker." I couldn't help laughing at my own dumb idea, half expecting him to tell me to shut up.

He snorted a laugh, and holy fuck, I was combusting in my seat.

"You're on Caye Caulker too?" he asked after a pause.

"Yeah," I said quickly.

"Two weeks at the Palms & Coral Resort, all-inclusive, courtesy of my sister—she was owed a favor and cashed it in for me. And you?"

"I'm there too. Courtesy of my sponsors. After my so-called breakout year." I rolled my eyes at myself. "Not that it was really a breakout year—I'm twenty-seven, not seventeen—but this is the year I finally got my shit together. Solid media attention, steady runs, actual wins. Hence 'breakout.' Not that you need to know all that."

"Cool."

"At least I've done well enough that my sponsors don't have to care I'm gay and worry about who I sleep with, only that I land the tricks." The words slipped out before my brain caught up, and panic coiled in my chest. Shit. Had I just said that out loud? "Can you ignore what I said? I'm not hitting on you or anything like that. Please don't hurt me, big guy." I was joking, but I must have seemed terrified or something, because he smiled, a flicker of compassion softening his face.

"It's okay," he said quietly, like he meant it, like I

didn't have to brace for impact. Jack closed the book fully, tone dry. "I'm bi, and also recently divorced."

What did I say? Should I be honest that I followed the hockey gossip sites as avidly as the ones for my own sport? "I read that. I'm sorry."

"It is what it is," he lied. I could see the pain in his beautiful eyes.

Then he tensed, seemed to go into his own world, frowned, and changed the subject. "So, we're in the same hotel," he finally said.

"Uh-huh," was all I could manage.

"Missed opportunity if you *weren't* hitting on me," he murmured.

"Huh?" Had I misheard? What in God's name had gone through Jack's thoughts to start a conversation that way? Was tall, built, and gorgeous hitting on me?

This time, his eyebrow raised in a way that spoke volumes. His expression shifted—speculative, assessing —as if he was really looking at me now. His gaze lingered, heavy enough that my skin prickled. Was it possible the Railers' captain was checking out the skinny-but-wiry snowboarder in the seat next to him? Heat coiled low in my gut, every nerve ending lighting up, and I was half hard just from the thought of Jack O'Leary's blue eyes fixed on me like that.

"My sister says they have all kinds of things lined up I can try—snorkeling, diving lessons, sunset catamaran cruises, zip-lining over the jungle, yoga on the beach, paddleboards, tours out to the reef."

"Uh-huh," I repeated, wriggling in my seat.

"She said the nightlife is quiet, though," he added. "Plenty of time to stay in bed." He was *definitely* leaning in, and I was *sure as hell* all the way hard now, thanking anyone who'd listen for the table that sat over my lap. "And sleep," he finished.

"Sleep. Yeah." Oh, brain, don't fail me now.

"Maybe, if I'm not reading this wrong, we make our own nightlife?"

Oh fuck.

THREE

Jack

STARING AT THIS BEAUTIFUL, YOUNGER MAN WHOM I'D
just hit on as if he were a nail and I a mallet, another
rush of pure lust flooded my brain. Which sent a
tsunami of blood to my dick, leaving my poor cerebral
matter drowning in a sea of desire. Not always a good
thing. Things that did not sound like me at all. *Make our
own nightlife? What the fuck?*

"I like the nightlife," he replied as the other
passengers began that maddening nonsense of freeing
themselves from their belts only to stand, bent over like
crones, in front of their seats. The clicking of hundreds
of seat belts floated forward to first class as the flight
crew waited for the ground crew to roll the jet bridge
into place.

"Do you like to boogie?" I asked and got a vacant
glance. Great. My affinity for Mom's seventies disco

tunes had made me seem even older than I felt at that moment. "It's a song. Alicia Bridges. Disco. My mother loved disco."

Jonathon Patrick Killian O'Leary. Shut the fuck up with the disco.

"Oh, cool," Tian replied, a hint of amusement on his too-pretty face.

"I personally don't remember the disco era." I felt I had to clarify in case he thought I was in my sixties rather than my late thirties.

Late, late, late *thirties.*

Fuck all the way off, me. I know how late my thirties are.

"My grandma thought they were pretty cool. She still has some bell-bottoms that she wears around on special days."

"Cool." The ache in my dick was lessening now that some of the lust juice in my skull was being replaced with reality. The plane door slid open. I felt the sudden need to exit stage left with as much speed as my creaky knees could muster. "Grandmas are cool. So are bell-bottoms. So, uhm, see you at the hotel then."

"Yeah," Tian replied, unsure now as I nearly checked the flight attendant off her little feet in my haste to get off this motherfucking plane as Sam Jackson might say if he were here.

If Sam Jackson were here, he would kick your ass for acting like a moron.

Yep, no doubt. I shot Tian a wobbly smile, apologized to the flight attendant, and with my carry-on in hand, sprinted off the plane with a "Thank you" to the young male flight attendant in front, saying goodbye. Jogging into the airport, I found the first men's room—next to a McDonald's—they really were everywhere—and rushed to the row of sinks. I splashed cold water on my face, rubbed it into my hair and beard, and then stood there staring at myself as my old friend self-doubt reared its ugly head.

You old, foolish ass. Look at yourself. As if that young stud was really interested in someone like you? Loser. Couldn't please his wife, couldn't lead his team to a victory, couldn't—

An incoming call thankfully pulled me from the spiral I was about to tumble into. My sister. I took the lifeline I knew her voice would bring me. Several men entered. The sound of flushing toilets and rushing water filled the air.

"Hey, you," I croaked as her pretty face came up on the lower corner of my phone screen. "You look snazzy."

"I know." She held her phone up a bit to show off her dark blue uniform dress, custom-fitted to her curves, a blue-and-gold scarf tied around her throat, and her hair tumbling down in thick waves of honey blonde and red.

"Damn, she's hot. You hitting that?" some random male next to me asked. I looked down at the guy, early forties, balding, pudgy, gawking at Fiona. His hands were soapy, his brow sweaty, and his skin tone the same color as school glue.

"Dude, that's my fucking sister," I snarled down at the man in the ugly suit.

"Oh, is she available for a date?" he asked, then wet his thin lips. I could hear my sister mumbling "Oh no" to herself.

"No, she is not. If I were you, buddy, I would move my ass down a few sinks before I decide that creeping into a private call then slobbering over a man's little sister is a drowning offense."

He gave Fiona a quick peek then slid down four sinks, hands still soapy. "I think I can still reach you," I warned, which helped spur him to leave the bathroom with lather on his hands. "Fucking creep."

"Jack," she said, then started to giggle.

"Sorry, not sorry. Jerks don't deserve to rinse their hands. So, can you talk? I need some help here."

"I have ten minutes before we take off for Tokyo, so can it be quick?"

"Shit, yeah, sorry. I just…" I turned back to face the mirror. "Okay, so I met this guy on the plane."

"Oh, did you? Tell me more!" Two men appeared, glancing at me, then attending to their handwashing as normal people should do.

I studied myself as I spoke. "He's really nice, super sexy, and way younger than me."

"Define way younger."

"Fiona, don't even go there. Twenty-seven."

"Okay, that's fine. Are you meeting him for drinks later?" She was fiddling with something in a plane galley as she spoke, her phone now propped up on a shelf, I assumed, aimed at her.

"No, I mean... maybe?" I ran a hand through my already messy hair. "He sat beside me, really charming, funny, he knew who I was, he's a fan..." I bumbled over things as they emerged into my thought stream. "We talked the whole flight. Then something came over me. Fiona, I swear, it was just like Father Fitzpatrick talks about. A demon took control of me, and I started saying things that I would never say. I hit on him hard. Said we should make our own nightlife. I just cannot with myself right now."

"Was he into you?"

"I think so. I mean... he said uh-huh a lot as I drooled over him. Oh shit. I'm as bad as the sweaty suit guy slobbering over a young, pretty thing way out of my league!" My eyes rounded as the realization of how rancid I must have sounded to Tian struck home.

"No, Jack, there is no way you could be—"

"I was though. Things fell out of me. It was a flyby possession. I knew I should have gone to confession before I left on this trip. Shit, Fiona."

"Jack, you hardly ever go to confession," she reminded me, her attention flicking from her phone to something in the distance. "My passengers are arriving. I have to go. Look, I know that what your ex-from-hell did to you knocked your self-confidence down some."

"Fiona—"

"Sure, her being a cheating bitch would ding your armor a bit, but you need to jump back on that horse— or sexy younger man—and get laid."

"I—"

"I have to go. Do not let this chance go by, Jack, or I'll kick you in the shin when I see you next. Promise me you'll go have fun with this guy, and in this case, fun means ample sloppy sex, and you will *not* go into full hermit mode."

"I promise," I lied, then had to say goodbye to my sister. I planned to go into major recluse mode as soon as I could find a cab to the hotel. If I never left my suite, I could never make a fool of myself in front of Tian. A man can have a lot of fun spending two weeks in his room. No shaving, no showering, room service. Who needs the sun or the surf or the sex? Not this guy.

TWO HOURS LATER, I WAS ENSCONCED IN MY LUXURY suite, gazing at the LGBTQ singles mixer kicking off four floors below by the pool. Around a hundred people were down there, enjoying cocktails, dancing, and getting to know each other, as the tropical breeze blew through the swaying palms. Dua Lipa's "Physical" floated up on the warm currents. I was in my boxers, a thin summer robe tied around my waist, on the patio sipping spring water from the fridge, waiting for my dinner to arrive from room service. The start of a perfect vacation was about to kick off as soon as my T-bone steak meal arrived. I had thought about Tian a few dozen times while unpacking. I'd even Googled him. He was popular. And good. Damn good. Lots of followers on Instagram and TikTok. And why not? The man oozed charm and sex appeal.

A soft knock on the door pulled me from the horny queers below. My stomach rumbled when I thought of the meal waiting outside. Steak, baked potatoes, green beans with almonds, a chocolate torte, and an icy cold bottle of beer. I'd settle down, watch some baseball, burp, scratch, and fart to my heart's content while the gyrating masses by the pool ended up feeling used and unloved come morning.

I yanked the door open, stared at the tray, and then glanced up when the door across the hall from mine opened. Tian filled the doorway, all tanned and gorgeous in some khaki shorts and a floral Hawaiian shirt showing off a nice expanse of strong chest. His calves were toned, thick with muscle, and his feet were in some cool leather sandals. Even his damned toes were sexy.

Our eyes met.

"Oh, hey, hi!" he said, closing the door behind him as I stood over my dinner like a mother bear protecting her cubs. "I was just heading down to the bar for a drink. Are you going to the mixer?"

Shit. Shit. Shit. "I uhm…"

"I mean, if you're going, I can wait for you," he said, a faint hint of hopefulness in his tone that made me forget all about steak and beer. He wanted me to go. Then his eyes dropped to the food at my bare feet. Feet that weren't as pretty as his. I'd broken a toe once after taking a puck to the boot, and it never healed quite right. It might have if I'd told the team doctor, but why bother? Not much to do with a broken toe. And it was the playoffs, so… "Or we can meet up at the pool after you eat?"

Somehow, and I'd discuss this with the parish priest after I get back to Harrisburg, that same lust demon grabbed control of my tongue.

"I'm done. I was just putting the empty dishes out. If you want to come in and wait while I shower quickly, we can go down and enjoy that nightlife," I said with such swagger that it surely had to be a foreign entity running my mouth.

"Sounds good," he said with a smile that made me hard instantly. I stepped back into my room, held the door open, and watched Tian enter my suite. With a sad sigh, I closed the door on my T-bone and double-stuffed baked potatoes. "Wow, this room is way nicer than mine. I mean mine's nice and all, but this is way bigger and looks out over the sea. I can only see the parking lot from my balcony."

He filled the room with a clean aura and fresh citrus scent. I wanted to get lost in his smell. Breathe it in, hold it in my lungs, and pass out while I held it in forever.

"My sister is a private flight attendant, so she knows all the good places, people, and things."

"Very cool," he said as he made his way to the balcony to gaze out over the setting sun painting the Caribbean. My cock throbbed with desire as he braced his arms on the railing, the movement pulling his shirt over his shoulders. His ass was divine. Tight and high, his shorts cradled those orbs lovingly. Bruno Mars' "24 K Magic" rolled up with a round of cheers that set his hips moving to the dance beat. I gulped.

"I'm going to shower," I called to him. He spun from the crowd that was hooting and bouncing below, to smile at me. "Would you like to wash my back?"

Father Fitzgerald, where are you when we need you?!

That monster filled with desperate craving throttled the tiny voice of sanity and salvation. Tian seemed uncertain for a moment. Then, slowly but deliberately, he stepped inside and closed the door to the patio.

"I did notice that the hotel forgot to include a back brush with the amenities."

He closed the distance, shedding that bright red and yellow flowery shirt as he neared. His chest was wide, not as broad as mine, or as hairy, but with a nice spattering of black hair that grew thicker as it led into the top of his shorts. Shorts that I noticed were tented. My dick was also at attention, poking outward to make a spectacle of itself as it held my boxers and robe out from my body. His gaze fell to it. I swallowed. He licked his lips. That slide of tongue over lower lip shredded whatever restraint I possessed. I reached for him, my fingers found the back of his neck, and I pulled him to me. He grunted at the impact, dark eyes flaring for a second before he rose to his toes to latch his mouth over mine. His fingers wound into my hair, my beard, my chest hair as our tongues tangled. Bold beyond reason, I cupped that sweet ass I'd just been admiring, gave both cheeks a hard squeeze, and moaned into his mouth at the groan that glute massage had earned me.

We stumbled into the bathroom, his mouth sealed to mine, my fingers kneading his ass. There wasn't much talking taking place. Mostly huffs, grunts, and breathy exhalations as we tore at each other's clothes. I was naked in no time. Tian, brash and young as he was, went to his knees to nuzzle my dick before I could turn the water on.

"Shit," I said, gazing at him as he licked my cockhead, the tip of his tongue dipping into the slit to gather a droplet lingering there. "Water is... damn it," I growled, grabbing the edge of the cool white counter as he took me down his throat with practiced ease. My toes curled at the sight of his nose buried in my ginger pubes. Off he came with a *pop*, his gaze touching mine. Sinful heat glowed in those dark eyes of his. "Such pretty lashes," I coughed and got a sweet smile.

"Such a fat cock," he sighed as he fumbled with the tie of his shorts. He leaned back, one hand on the base of my dick, the other loosening a tan string, to allow me to see his cock when he fished it out. Long but girthy with a slight list to the left. My mouth watered. And it was not for the steak sitting in the corridor getting cold. "Will you come down my throat?"

"Christ above," I mumbled, then nodded. With a grin, he went down on me with gusto. He knew how to suck dick, that was for sure, because he had me teetering on the edge in no time. "Been a while…. slow down… oh shit." He seemed to have turned a deaf ear to me as he sucked hard and fast, his fist pumping away on his own dick. My balls contracted, spun afire, and I thrust deep to empty myself on his tonsils. Just as he asked. "Fuck, shit, shit, fuck."

He wrung me out, swallowing each pulse of cum, until I was shaking like a drum head. When he leaned back to rest on his heels, I watched through hazy, sated eyes as he spat some cum and saliva onto his own dick to finish himself off. With a few strokes of a tight fist, he shot all over his hand, my toes, and the floor. It took every ounce of sanity I was holding on to—and that wasn't much at this point—to stop myself from falling to the floor to clean his spunk from the tiles with my tongue. Instead, I pulled him to his feet, gazes locked, and lifted his cum-coated hand to my lips.

He said nothing but his eyes, pupils already blown, watched with heated interest as I lapped the seed from his fingers. After his palm was clean, he kissed me hard, smearing my taste and his together. It was fucking divine. And the singular most erotic moment of my life.

My stomach chose that moment to snarl. Tian broke the kiss to look down, then back at me.

"I may have lied about having dinner," I confessed, kissing his fingertips while my gut gurgled hungrily. "Want to share a steak?"

He smiled wantonly. "After that shower? We both could use one before whatever is next." He leaned in. "Do you have condoms?"

Oh. Oh shit, there was a round two to come. Holy hell. I was beginning to think that I might have been wrong about being a hermit in paradise.

FOUR

Tian

I WAS STILL BUZZING FROM SUCKING HIM DOWN IN THE bathroom, my lips tingling, my throat raw in the best way, and we never made it to the steak. Jack's body dwarfed mine, big hands and heavy muscle, and when he lifted me up as if I weighed nothing, I clung to him as heat curled low in my belly.

"I want you inside me."

"Not steak?" he asked, and fake-pouted, although his jokey tone didn't match the apparent reluctance to let me go.

"Now." I was happy to beg.

He paused, his breath rough at my ear. "Negative, PrEP. Condoms."

"Same. Safe's the only way I play," I whispered, pressing my forehead to his, heart racing.

He kissed me once, slow and deliberate, before

hoisting me up. I wrapped my legs around his waist, and he freaking carried me to his bed. I kind of hoped he'd toss me, but no, he was a gentleman, and he set me down gently, then fumbled inside a wash bag for foil packets and a small tube, tossing them between us. My breath caught when he caged me. I'd had him in my mouth, I knew it was thicker than anyone I'd ever taken, and my body clenched in anticipation. This could be the worst pain or the best freaking thing to ever happen to me.

"Tell me if it's too much," he said, voice low.

"I want all of it," I answered, firmer than I thought I could manage.

The first slide of his slick fingers worked me open, patient, careful, stretching me until I writhed against the sheets, moaning into his mouth when he bent to kiss me. He whispered over my lips, filthy praise tumbling out between gentle reassurances—telling me how tight I was, how gorgeous I looked spread out for him, how he wanted to ruin me and worship me in the same breath. He sat back on his knees, fingers still inside me, his free hand teasing over my chest, finding my nipples, rolling one between his fingers until I arched into him with a whimper. He pinched lightly, soothed with a thumb, then tugged again, alternating pleasure and sting until I was gasping, my cock leaking against my stomach. Each curl of his fingers had me begging louder, kissing him back hungrily, tasting the salt of his sweat as he called me perfect, beautiful, brave, until I was shaking and pleading for more.

"Look at you opening up for me," he murmured, kissing the corner of my mouth, then my jaw, then the hollow of my throat. "So beautiful, Tian. Taking my fingers like you were made for me." His voice was rough, praise spilling from him, dirty and reverent all at once. I moaned into his kisses, clutching his shoulders as he worked me wider, whispering promises that he'd give me everything, that I'd never forget how it felt to be filled by him. Each filthy word made my cock leak, every gentle press of his lips steadying me even as I begged for more.

"Now, Jack. Now. Please, I need you," I begged, my voice raw with urgency.

He stared down at me with something like surprise, as if he couldn't quite believe how desperate I was for him, how badly I wanted him inside me. His hesitation made me hold him tighter, tilting up for another kiss, showing him with every gasp and wordless plea that I craved all of him, right now.

I begged when he hesitated, and when he finally rolled the condom down his length and pressed the tip in, waiting for me to relax, the world narrowed to the heat and stretch of him filling me, inch by glorious inch. My breath broke on a cry, half pleasure, half disbelief someone this big could fit inside me. But he carried me through it, murmuring encouragement, his chest pressed to mine, his strength surrounding me.

"Tell me I'm not hurting you, please," he groaned, his forehead pressed to mine, eyes searching. He winced when I cried out, but I cupped his face and kissed him hard, reassuring.

"So, fucking good, Jack. You're perfect. Don't stop."

"I don't want to hurt you," he said again, voice breaking, almost desperate. "Please don't let me—"

I moved then, grinding up against him, my nails raking down his back, forcing his eyes wide. "Move, Jack," I panted. "Move." When he bottomed out, my toes curled. "Fuck," I gasped, nails biting into his back. "Fuck!"

"You good?" he asked, sweat beading on his temple.

"Better than good. Move."

He did. Long, slow thrusts that stole my sanity, building a rhythm that had me meeting him eagerly. Every push lifted me closer to the edge, his weight grounding me, my cock trapped between us, delicious friction with every thrust, rubbing against the ridges of his abs and the coarse hair on his belly, making me cry out as his mouth silenced my moans with desperate kisses. I was lost in him—his size, his strength, the way he seemed to hold all of me and give me everything back.

When release tore through me, it was with his name

on my lips, my body clenching hard around him, dragging his climax out of him with a guttural growl. He buried himself deep, trembling as the condom caught the heat of him. He stayed there, holding me, kissing me softly as we both came down, until I could only sigh and collapse under him, utterly undone.

"Fuck, that was…"

"Okay?" he asked, and there was that fear back in his tone, as if he needed reassurance.

He eased himself out as he asked, and I rolled with him to lie on top of his broad chest. He let me sprawl there, his big hands rubbing lazy circles over my back. I took my time kissing him deeply, then pressed my forehead to his.

"That was the best casual limited-time on an island fuck I've ever had," I confessed, breath still shaky.

"You have a lot of casual limited-time on an island fucks?" he asked.

"Nope." I kissed the skin I could reach. "Your cock is fucking amazing, and what you do with it… Wow."

"Really?" Christ, he sounded so doubtful.

I lifted my head, searching his face. His expression was shadowed, a wince flickering across his features. Had someone told him otherwise? Maybe his ex? Or other hookups like me? The thought made my chest tighten. I stroked his jaw gently, willing him to believe me. "Someone did a number on you, didn't they?"

"No, I…" He closed his eyes again. "I don't want to hurt you."

"Shit, Jack, you're perfect," I murmured, kissing him again, sealing the words with my mouth. "I'm going to enjoy every single second of the next two weeks with you—every kiss, every touch, every time we fuck until neither of us can move."

"You want to do this again?" Again, doubt flickered in his eyes, as if he couldn't quite believe I'd want him again. I hated that. I'd prove it to him, show him what I craved, and if that wasn't enough, I'd tell him outright until he understood.

I chuckled, then buried my face into his neck and hung on like a limpet.

"Yep, you, me, tangled up together for fourteen days straight—sex, sweat, kisses, every filthy, perfect thing we can cram into the best damn holiday hookup ever. Then home. Work. Win."

"Yeah," he said on a sigh. "Best hookup ever."

BY DAY TWO, WE GAVE UP ON THE IDEA OF ME HAVING my own room and shoved all my things into the corner of his suite. By the end of that second day, I had closet space—my riot of bright colors hanging beside his neat rows of navy and gray—and by the start of day three, we were already making a run for more condoms and so much lube I doubted the island had any left. Maybe I was exaggerating, but I couldn't get enough of him. We took each other everywhere—on the cool tiled floor when we couldn't make it to the bed, over the arm of the sofa, half-submerged in the bath, and once he even had me braced against the shower door, slippery with oil from the couples massage we'd booked on a whim. Not that we were officially a couple, but two-for-one was too good to pass up, and the way he kissed me before and after, I could almost believe we were.

Not sure how that would work. I didn't do relationships—I never had. I'd always been focused on one thing and one thing only: securing a spot on the Olympic team, pushing myself harder than anyone else, X Games gold, being the best. That was the plan, the dream, the only thing that mattered. Everything else— dating, hookups, messy feelings—was just noise in the background. Or at least, that was what I told myself. But lying in Jack's arms last night, his heartbeat steady under my ear, I wasn't so sure anymore. Somehow, without me even realizing it, he was slipping past every wall I'd built in my battle to get to the top of my game, prying open the locked doors, making me want more than just sex and gold medals. He was working his way under my defenses, and the scariest part was at that moment, right there, I didn't want to stop him.

"I'm not sure about this," he said for the tenth time as we stood on the sand with boards tucked under our arms. We were going surfing—something I'd done a few times before. Not a whole lot of surfing in Colorado, where I grew up, and I hadn't had many chances since—training, competitions, always on the mountain instead of the beach. I had some transferable skills from snowboarding, enough balance and awareness of edges to make me decent on a board, but he was adamant he'd be down and out in seconds, convinced the ocean would eat him alive.

This was Jack's first time, and the way he eyed the rolling waves made me grin.

"Come on, big guy, you strap knives to your feet and face down guys who want to knock you into next week. You can handle a board and some water."

"Why can't we just go snorkeling again?" he asked, a little desperate, shifting his board under his arm as if it might bite him, eyes flicking to the waves as if they were plotting his demise. The way his voice cracked made me laugh, but there was a kind of boyish charm in how the big, fearless Railers' captain was so wary of a surfboard.

We paddled out together, me cutting through the water while Jack wobbled on his board, shoulders tight with tension. "Relax," I called over, water dripping into my mouth as I grinned at him. "It's just like skating— find your balance, trust your stance."

He muttered something about preferring to face down a six-foot defenseman, but he followed me anyway, powerful arms pulling through the surf. When we reached the break, I showed him how to turn the board nose into the swell, how to feel the lift before pushing up. "Don't think about it too much—just ride it like you own it," I encouraged, steadying his board when it rocked.

When the first small wave came, I popped up easily, riding it for a few seconds before splashing back into the water. Jack tried, legs stiff, arms pinwheeling, and he toppled with a shout and a splash. I laughed so hard I almost lost my own board. He surfaced, sputtering, glaring at me, but there was a spark of laughter in his eyes too. "Again," he growled.

Each time he clambered back on his board and tried again, a swell of pride rose in my chest. It wasn't just that he was willing to keep going; it was the determined set of his jaw, the way his laugh broke through his frustration, and how damn good he looked out here in the sun, dripping and fierce. My heart kicked harder than the waves beneath us. Affection welled up alongside the pride, sharp and unexpected, leaving me grinning like an idiot as I watched him paddle out for another try.

This was supposed to be a hookup. Fourteen days of freedom, bodies and heat and nothing more, before the grind started again. This wasn't meant to be some fairytale, no white picket fences or promises whispered under the stars. And yet, watching him fight the ocean with that stubborn grin, feeling my chest ache with pride and something that felt dangerously like longing, I couldn't stop the thought that maybe—just maybe—it could become more than I'd planned.

We ended by pushing out far enough to sit on the boards and talk. The waves rocked us gently as we straddled our boards, catching our breath.

"So, tell me more about Tian," Jack asked—the first time he'd done so in the days we'd been sharing a bed.

"Tian-Lei," I corrected with a smile, our knees knocking as a swell pushed us together for a moment. "Tian-Lei Cai-Wilder, to be exact. My birth name was Cai Tian Lei—Cai is the family name, so it came first. Tian Lei means heavenly thunder." I smirked then and gestured at my small build. "Not so much thunder as a sparkler in a storm, all flash and noise but not much weight," I joked.

Jack smiled faintly, the corners of his eyes soft. "Heavenly thunder suits you more than you think," he said. "You come crashing in, full of energy, light up everything around you. Don't sell yourself short."

I made a show of fluttering my eyelashes. "Aww, he likes me."

He tugged the strap attached to my ankle, dragging my board closer until our knees bumped again, then leaned over to kiss me, salt water still on his lips. "Yeah," he murmured, eyes locked on mine. "I like you." My chest constricted so tight it was hard to breathe, and for once, I didn't need to joke or hide behind words—I just kissed him back.

A little dazed when we separated, it took me a moment to get back on track. "Uhm, so my adoptive parents kept my Chinese name, even hyphenated it, so for a while I was Tian-Lei Cai. When I turned twelve, I wanted more control over who I was, and I chose to add their last name too because they were my parents and I loved them and I wanted so hard to be a Wilder—so now I'm Tian Cai-Wilder. Most people just call me Tian, though."

For once, I wasn't blurting things out like I usually did. Being here with him, after seeing Jack let go and laugh at himself in the surf, I felt… comfortable. Safe enough to open up.

"How old were you when they adopted you?"

"A baby, ten months old. No one knows who my birth parents were—I was left on the doorstep of an orphanage one night, wrapped in a blanket with nothing else. The Wilders flew halfway across the world to bring me home. I've never forgotten what they gave up, what they risked, just to make me their son."

"So, you don't know anything about your birth parents?" He looked adorably awkward. "Shit, should I ask you that?"

I shrugged. "I'm an open book," I lied. "I could find them if I wanted, I guess. Mom and Dad said they'd support me if I wanted to, but I don't. I don't need to.

Someone out there gave me life, sure, but my parents—the ones who held me when I cried, who stood on frozen mountains cheering me on, who sacrificed so much for me—that's who matters. Going back would feel like betraying them, like saying they weren't enough. And they are. They're everything. So no, I don't intend to connect with my birth parents. My life is with Mei and Ben Wilder, and my little sister Li Hua, also adopted... with the family who chose me and never let go."

"They sound like good people."

"They are, and they never let me forget my cultural roots—made sure I learned Mandarin basics, celebrated Lunar New Year with me every year, and cooked Sichuan dishes even if they weren't perfect. They wanted me to know where I came from, even as they gave me a home and a future." I grinned. "What about you?"

"Oh, I have a younger sister too, her name is Fiona. My folks both died in a car crash a few years ago. We were all pretty tight. Dad and Mom were great hockey parents, and just great parents in general. Fi and I are super close. She kind of likes to run my life. She hates my ex and takes great joy in reminding me how lucky I am to be rid of her. Which now that I've met you I'm starting to believe." His eyes widened as if he'd revealed too much.

"I'm guessing she's an ex for a reason."

"Yeah," he said tiredly. He hadn't mentioned her

since confirming the divorce on the plane, and I wasn't going to push. "So how did you get into snowboarding?"

Good change of subject, Mr. Hockey Star.

"We lived in Breckenridge, close to Keystone and Copper, some of the best snowboarding centers in Colorado. I wasn't tall enough to play basketball, quick enough for track, or big enough for football, but shit, I was good on the beginner boards. Then I became obsessed."

"I read that you won a gold medal in the X-Games," Jack said, almost shyly.

"You been looking me up?" I teased.

"Well, you know a lot about my career, so I thought it was only fair."

"It's taken me years to get there," I admitted, eyes on the horizon. "Years of falling, breaking bones, clawing my way back."

"So now you have the gold, what's next?"

"Bigger, better tricks. There's this one I've been dreaming about—a cab triple cork with a late nose grab into a fourteen-forty, clean and landed without a wobble. No one's pulled it off in competition yet. It's dangerous as hell, the kind of thing that could make my career or break my body, but I can't stop thinking about it."

He frowned. "Breaking your body doesn't sound good."

"Says the hockey star."

"True."

"Then the Olympics. Shit, everything I do now is about one thing only—earning a place on the Olympic team, chasing gold. My parents gave up so much so I could chase snow and speed instead of stability. I owe them everything, and I owe myself too. Every ounce of powder I carve, every trick I land—it's for them as much as for me. It's everything to me. I can't let them down. I can't let myself down." My voice cracked, but I didn't look away.

Wow, that got very deep very quickly.

Jack was quiet for a long beat, then gave a small, almost wry smile. "I get that. I've never been chosen for the US team. Not once. But you know what? I'm good with that. I've got my place. I'm captain of the Railers. That's more than enough for me." Then he grinned. "I'll watch you in the Olympics and remember us floating here as you land the late nose cork grab land thing."

And I grinned back. "I'll wave at you as I'm doing it."

FIVE

Jack

TIAN WAS GIVING ME THE ODDEST OF GLANCES AS IF HE couldn't quite believe his eyes.

Such pretty eyes they were…

"Where did you get this idea?" he asked as he circled the two black mountain bikes waiting for us outside the front door of the hotel.

"The desk clerk who helped us with our dinner suggestions and the snorkeling reservations for tomorrow?" He nodded, lowering his designer shades to peer at me with amusement in his eyes. "She mentioned this when you were in the bathroom, so I reserved two bikes."

"Are they e-bikes?" He knelt to inspect the bikes for motors.

"No, lazy butt, they're fully powered by leg muscles. I'm sure I can pedal around the island for a day but if you're scared you can't keep up with an old man…" I let that dangle, knowing full well his competitive nature would never let him back down from a challenge.

"Okay, first off, as if." He straightened then threw a muscular leg over the bike seat. "Secondly, the reason I asked about them being e-bikes is because this is a vacation. Va-kay-shun. We're supposed to be relaxing and having lots of sex while making terrible food decisions. Do you know how to relax off the ice?"

I crossed my arms over my pale blue tank with a tribal design swimming sea turtle. "You're one to talk. You never stop moving. Even when you're asleep you're twitching like a dog dreaming of catching a rabbit."

"Bow-wow." He leaned in, stole a kiss, and then drove his heel into the kickstand. Off he sped, veering left to avoid running into an older couple and their bags.

"Cheater." I chuckled then rushed to get my ass on that bike seat and start pedaling. I caught up fast.

"Hey there good-looking," he called as we began our trek. The Caribbean was to his right with the sun sparkling off the waves. Warm wind blew through his hair. He was so vibrant, so alive, so stunning in his youth and vigor. And he was my lover. Go fucking figure.

"Don't try to sweet talk me, you pumpkin eater."

He laughed. The ride slowed a bit then to just drink

in the isolated beauty all around us. There were no cars on Caye Caulker, just some golf carts serving as taxis or rentals for those unwilling or unable to bike or walk. Despite his accusations of me not knowing how to chill, I knew how to relax. I was embracing the go-slow mentality of the island as well as I could. The day stretched ahead of us with no schedules, no morning skates, no pressers, no agents. Just Tian and me. Our first stop to rest and rehydrate, as the temps were climbing, was along a marina. Several dozen boats bobbed on the crystal blue water as we walked our bikes to a shady little café. It was early so the outside eatery was empty save for a pelican that had decided to sit on a rail to study anyone entering the thatched area.

Tian took a dozen selfies of himself and the pelican while I ordered us some bottles of water and a snack. The barkeep talked me into trying some fry jacks, which he touted to be the best on the island. I nodded, paid, and returned to a table in the shade where I toed off my sneakers so I could sink my toes into the sand.

Tian was seated a few feet from the pelican, now engaged in conversation with the seabird. "Among your skills on the snow and in bed, you also speak fluent bird?" I asked while passing over a cold bottle of spring water.

"My skills are vast and varied," he replied with a wink. I could attest that he did have some wicked expertise with that mouth of his. "Winifred and I were just discussing how she is a brown pelican, as evidenced by her white head, dark body, and gold neck. She told me that her throat pouch is three times larger than her stomach, which is quite advantageous as she swallows the fish and crustaceans she catches whole."

"Winifred?" I asked after emptying half my bottle of water. Tian nodded, a gust of wind off the bright blue sea tossing his hair into his face. "Winifred told you all of that, or was it Google?"

He gasped. "Jack, I'm shocked that you would doubt my avian chat ability!"

"Sorry, I'll never question your bird whispering talents again."

Tian sniffed, then chuckled. Our snack arrived then. We both stared at the fried dough triangles stacked on our plates, topped with cheese and refried beans.

"I thought they'd be like doughnuts," I confessed after the bartender returned to setting up his bar for the busy lunch crush ahead.

"If we eat all these beans, we'll have extra speed to propel us along," Tian offered while Winifred walked down the railing to glance over his shoulder at his food. He shot the bird a look, then tossed a fry jack to her. She caught it with a snap. "Okay, this bird has begged off people before," Tian said, to which I bobbed my head.

We dove into our breakfasts with gusto. The food was delicious. The pastry light and airy, the cheese spicy and gooey, and the refried beans creamy and savory. It was a filling meal, and after we fed Winifred the final fry jack on my plate, we left a nice tip and waved at the bartender and the pelican. Back on our bikes, we then rode out to the Split, an iconic spot where the island splits in two, with a canal dividing the two parts. There were bars aplenty here, but we skipped them as we were still stuffed from our breakfast. Onward we rode, chatting, laughing at dumb jokes the other made about passing gas, giving us bursts of speed.

The day slipped by quickly from our lunch at a hopping island bar where you could drink and eat at a submerged table sitting in the turquoise ocean. It was quite an experience eating our shrimp kabobs while the sea lapped at our calves. Then we took off once more, pedaling through an area rich with shops and art galleries. Tian and I spent several hours shopping in the various stores. We both ended up purchasing some small oils done in vibrant colors by local artists to take home with us. Mine was a beautiful rendition of a sea turtle in tones of purple and blue, and Tian found a small oil in a wooden frame with a woman's face done in vivid oranges and yellows. Both would fit in our suitcases, so we had them shipped to the hotel.

As evening came, we found ourselves sitting outside once more, on a pier where you could eat a gourmet meal while watching stingrays idling, gliding by under the wharf. The sun was mere inches above the horizon, streaking the sky with pinks, blues, and violets. "Adore

You" by Harry Styles wafted outside to dance on the evening tide. Tian was leaning back in his chair, eyes closed, the sunset tinting his face with subtle paintbrush strokes of indigo.

"Would you like to dance?" I asked out of nowhere because I was no great shakes at dancing. I could count how many times I'd been on a dance floor on one hand, and one of those times was my wedding. Whatever possessed me to ask, I had no clue, but his sleepy eyes opened, and his gaze met mine.

"I would like that a lot," he replied. The wharf wasn't built for dancing, the tables were close, but without a further thought of how I'd probably step on his toes or fall off the wooden dock into the water, I took his hand and stood.

My ass bumped the edge of the table as he melted into my arms. I cupped his sandy cheeks, bringing his lips flavored by the Hudut–Garifuna fish cooked in coconut broth and served with plantains, which he'd had for his evening meal. His tongue held the sweet and spicy taste as I licked into his mouth with a soft, slow intention. I was feeling things. Things leading me to know that this supposedly casual affair with Tian was different. Deep. Not just a sex fling, no matter what rational-Jack demanded, emotional-Jack called it. He was always responsive, and this kiss was no different, but the mad chaotic heat was lessened. Perhaps because we were surrounded by people trying to eat their dinners. Maybe the lust that seemed to have been driving us over the past few days was abated for the time being. We'd been going at it like oversexed rabbits since our chance meeting at my hotel room door.

Whatever the reason, swaying back and forth, his lips on mine, this moment was one of those lasting memories. The one thing that when you hear a song or smell an aroma, or taste a food, it brings you right back to that place in time.

"You want to know something funny?" I asked when the kiss broke, and his head came to rest on my shoulder.

"Yeah," he replied groggily, kiss-drunk, belly full, he was pliable as a warm wax. He smelled of sun, sand, and man.

"I can't dance," I admitted as he moved in perfect syncopation with my less than graceful moves. Sways was the correct terminology. He swayed in time with me.

"No one is good at everything," he whispered as he nosed at my exposed clavicle then dropped a kiss to the protruding bone. "I think you're doing just fine. You want to know something?"

"Yeah," I answered, my hands on his hips, the sun dropping out of sight as workers began lighting tiki torches around us. No one told us to stop dancing in the aisle, so we kept rocking gently back and forth.

"I never liked Harry Styles until now." He chuckled. "Whenever I hear this song, I'll think of this day."

"Yeah, me too," I replied. I'd remember a lot more of this getaway than just this one day. I'd recall it all and bask in each recollection as a cat lounges in a sunbeam. And yes, I was sure I would purr while doing so...

SIX

Tian

BACK AT THE HOTEL, JACK AND I HEADED STRAIGHT FOR
our room. The lobby was buzzing with late-night
chatter, but we barely noticed as we were too wrapped
up in each other. In the elevator we pressed close,
kissing long and lazily as the numbers ticked upward,
every *ding* of the floor making my pulse race. By the
time we reached our level, his hand was already warm at
the small of my back, guiding me down the hallway. At
the door, we paused for another kiss, deeper, lingering,
before stumbling inside where the world narrowed down
to just us.

And when we made love, it was slow and sweet.

But when it was done, despite the high of the day
still buzzing in my veins, the air shifted. When he
came out of the bathroom wrapped in a towel, as I was
getting water from the refrigerator, he was quiet,

sitting on the edge of the bed, rubbing a hand over his face.

"You okay?" I asked, tugging my shirt over my head.

"Yeah, it's been the most perfect day," he said, glancing up at me as though he needed me to confirm it.

"Agreed," I said, dropping down beside him. "Perfect."

He lay back on the bed and stretched his limbs like a starfish.

I trailed my fingers along his thigh and paused when I noticed a pale scar cutting across his knee. "How'd you get this?" I asked softly.

Jack sighed, his hand coming down to brush over the mark, fingers lingering as if he could still feel the impact. His shoulders hunched a little, the easy strength in his body giving way to something guarded. I felt the heat of the scar under my fingertips, the raised line against his skin, and in that small touch I saw evidence of all the battles he'd fought to keep playing. He looked away as he spoke, eyes distant, as if he were back on the ice reliving it, like it still ached. "Training camp, years ago. Took a hit in practice, tore it up bad. Surgery, months of rehab. Thought it might be the end back then." He glanced at me, eyes shadowed. "But it wasn't." He huffed out a laugh without humor. "I fought my way back. Still fighting, every day."

Something about his tone made me pause. He

sounded almost regretful, as if the memory still weighed on him even though he'd fought his way back. For a second, I wondered if the scars on his body were etched into him in other ways too. I held my tongue, sensing he was working up to something and not wanting to interrupt.

"Sometimes I'm just tired."

"You work hard," I reminded him.

"Yeah, but not just that. I forget I have enough money to retire on if I wanted, but sometimes…"

"What?" I sat on the edge of the bed.

"Some days… it feels like I've been 'Captain O'Leary' forever. Like that's all I am. The captain. The guy who never breaks." His shoulders sagged. "And I'm not twenty anymore. Hell, some mornings my knees remind me I'm closer to the end than the start."

I leaned down and kissed his hair, trying to lighten what he was saying. "You still skate circles around half the league."

"Doesn't feel like it," he muttered.

I brushed it off then, but later those words stuck, burrowing under my skin. I was just coming into my highs—the medals, the chance to maybe make Team USA for the Olympics, the adulation, the new money from sponsors—while he was already talking like his life in sport was winding down. It underlined how different our journeys were, me just climbing the mountain while he was looking down from the other side, wondering how much longer he could keep going.

To fill the silence, I admitted something myself. "It's lonely out there sometimes. People think all the travel and sponsors are glamorous. They don't see the airports at three a.m. or the hotels where you don't know anyone. Feels like I'm always moving, never home."

"You're young enough to thrive on it, Tian," he said quietly. "I'm just… gah… old."

"You're not old," I shot back, brushing my thumb over his cheek. "You just hit your prime earlier than I did, and now you get to think about what's next."

"I don't know what's next," he admitted. "I have two years left on my contract, and I… do I even have that in me? Some mornings I wonder." He let out a shaky laugh. "And then I think, fuck yes I do. It's just— it takes more work now. More time to keep up. More energy to see things through."

"Do you think we'll see each other after this?" The words came out halting, my throat dry. My palms were damp, and I couldn't quite meet his eyes. Part of me wanted to bite the question back, afraid of hearing no, afraid of seeing pity on his face. But I needed to know, even if the answer gutted me. "Would you want to? I mean, I could visit Harrisburg, and when you play Denver you could look me up… y'know." Jeez, I couldn't even put it into words.

"Part of me wants to," Jack murmured. "But we can't."

"We can't?"

"We said we'd have the two weeks; it's for the best."

I wanted to argue; I thought I saw hesitation in his expression. Maybe he wanted to argue with himself, but then I nodded, my chest tight. "I get that."

His gaze went soft for a moment, but then he shook his head. "I mean, what even would it look like back in the real world? It wouldn't be bike rides and sunsets and dancing, it would be... ships passing in the night." He frowned at his analogy, and it made me smile.

"I know."

"That's why this can't go anywhere, Tian. Look, I'm not trying to be negative, and I don't want to sound miserable, but I need to be honest. I have to go back and work hard on myself—my body, my game. And you're so close to making Team USA, you're at the top of your game."

"From your lips," I muttered.

"You can't let yourself get distracted, not now. I needed this reset with you, but when the season starts, it's everything. And I know you'll be just as busy, chasing comps and medals. We'd barely see each other. That's not fair to either of us."

I opened my mouth to argue, but his reasoning was sound. He wasn't pushing me away because he didn't care; he was trying to be realistic. Still, it stung.

I swallowed hard, my voice cracking as I blurted, eyes fixed anywhere but on him too desperate and too raw to hold it back, "It's lonely out there sometimes. Even with all the travel, all the sponsorship perks... it's lonely. It'd be nice to have a friend that—"

Jack cut in quickly, almost too quickly. "—that what? Meets up every so often to hook up, then leaves?"

The words hit me like a punch. I flinched, hurt sharp in my chest. "I didn't say that. I didn't mean... shit."

There was regret in his eyes, but the damage was done. My throat worked around words I couldn't quite form, the air heavy between us.

"I get it," I said, even if every part of me hated agreeing.

I curled into his side, pressing my face against his chest, listening to the steady beat of his heart. He wrapped an arm around me, his lips brushing the top of my hair, and I kissed the warm skin at his throat. We clung to each other as if we could stop the night from ending. But underneath the sweetness of the kisses and the warmth of his embrace, I knew the truth—that when morning came, we'd be heading in different directions, pretending it was all okay.

THE NEXT MORNING, I WOKE FIRST AND SPENT THE longest time staring at Jack's face, weighing everything in my head—gold medals and glory on one side, the man in front of me on the other. My mind spun through possible futures: standing on Olympic podiums, sponsors cheering my name, or walking away from everything I'd battled through to build a life with him. Neither path was easy, and the ache in my chest told me both mattered more than I wanted to admit. The early sun filtered through the gauzy curtains at the windows, laying shadows across his skin, catching on the rough stubble of his jaw. There was utter peace in his expression as he slept, the kind that made my chest ache with wanting to freeze this moment forever. wondering if the chance at Olympic gold, at success, was worth more than this.

More than what?

My rational side kicked in—I absolutely hated my rational side. We'd shared sex and connection filled with fun and laughter, capturing idyllic moments that weren't part of normal life. Yet here I was, making it seem like more than it could ever be, and I knew I was blowing it out of proportion. I knew what we needed to do.

My parents had sacrificed so much to get me to the level I was at—early mornings driving me to the slopes, scraping together money for equipment and travel, holding their breath every time I fell hard and got back up again. I'd given up everything to be here too: friendships, normal school life, a chance at anything resembling stability. And now I was lying here thinking what? That a two-week fling, however perfect, was worth more than all of that? The thought twisted in my gut, made me feel selfish and reckless, but also desperate because some small, dangerous part of me whispered maybe it was.

I wanted this.

I couldn't have this.

I shouldn't want this.

Jack stirred, then woke and smiled at me, the smile wavering as the realization of the end of this hit him as hard as it hit me.

"Shower?" he asked. We brushed our teeth, kissed between mouthfuls of toothpaste, held hands, touched every chance we got, as if we could make up for all the time we were about to lose.

In the shower, it started with a gentle kiss, the hot spray pounding over our shoulders and trickling down our skin. The steam clung to us, the tiles slick beneath our feet, and the scent of soap and heat filled the small space. Water ran down his chest and over mine as our mouths met, slippery skin pressed tight, every sensation heightened by the warmth surrounding us. Then his hands slid over my shoulders, down my back, pulling me close until our bodies lined up.

It wasn't frantic this time, not desperate—just slow, quiet goodbyes written in skin and steam. I pressed into him, frotting against his thigh as he rocked against me, every movement matched, every sigh caught in a kiss.

My fingers tangled in his wet hair, his lips brushing over mine, over my jaw, down my throat. The heat built gradually, tender and inevitable, until we both shuddered, clinging to each other as if the water might wash us apart. When it was over, we stayed wrapped together, foreheads touching, trading gentle kisses under the spray, neither of us willing to let go first.

We dried off slowly, deliberately, as though dragging out the minutes could somehow stall time itself. He handed me a towel with a crooked smile, and I smoothed it over his shoulders, memorizing the curve of muscle beneath my palms. Even then we kept touching —brushing fingers, lingering glances in the mirror—as if letting go would make the goodbye too real. Every small gesture carried weight, each kiss to damp skin a promise neither of us dared speak aloud.

It was goodbye.

SEVEN

Jack

THE DREADED MOMENT HAD ARRIVED.

Tian and I were flying out of paradise this morning. Him back to Colorado. Me to Harrisburg. Both of us had training for our respective sports. The Railers and I had a lot of fine-tuning to do, and the only way to come into the season ready to kick ass was to train. Hard. Harder than I ever had before. I was old. The rest of the team was not so old. If I didn't perform well, I'd be let go. No disrespect to the Railers organization as that was the business. You don't bring the Cup home; you're on the block. Happens every year to players, coaches, and general managers. I was nothing special.

So, if I wanted to stay in hockey, and some mornings I wondered if I really did, given all the aches and pains, I had to intensify my pre-season prep. What would I do if I didn't play hockey? I had nothing in my life other than my sister and this brief fourteen-day holiday that had given me a tiny window into happiness with another person. Now the window was closing. Again.

"You've been staring at your underwear for a long time," Tian commented. I glanced across the rumpled bed to where his case sat snapped and ready to roll. From his intense expression I knew he was trying to figure out where I was mentally. "You okay?

"Yeah, I'm good. Just thinking about getting back on the ice. Training and all that." I closed the lid on my case, smiled widely, and zipped it shut. "When is your flight again?"

He glanced at his phone after giving me a curious glance. "About two hours."

"Right, right." I'd blocked that departure time from my head. "I guess you'd best get rolling then. Your ride will be waiting for you."

"Yeah, I guess." He hoisted his bag from the bed.

I stood and watched him pad around in fancy sneakers, shorts, and a tee. A gorgeous specimen of a young man in his prime. And he'd been mine. For two weeks. For some reason this sexy-as-sin athlete had wanted to not only fondle my old man balls but suck them until I blew sky high like a Roman candle. He dropped his bags by my feet. My plane back to Harrisburg was at four. I had time to kill. Alone. Sitting by the pool with a drink in hand. Ugh. "This has been amazing." He cupped my hairy face in his strong hands, dark eyes melancholy. "I wish we had more time but…"

"Yeah I wish so too. Damn buts. Can I kiss you goodbye?"

"You better." He rose to his toes.

I enveloped him in a hug that pushed some air from his lungs as our mouths met. I licked over his tongue, picking up the sharp taste of spearmint toothpaste as I breathed in the warm scent of his skin mingling with his cologne. I wanted to lock the sensory memory down so I could pull it up when I thumbed through the few dozen selfies we had snapped during our stay.

"I'm going to miss you. If you're ever in Colorado and I'm there… not that I'm there in the season… but hell, look me up."

"I will," I whispered then, as hard as it was, I released him.

He held my face for a moment longer, then forced a smile. "Maybe we'll run into each other then."

I nodded, and his hands fell from my face. I wanted to say things to him. Lots of things. But this was what we had agreed on. A clean break. We'd come into this knowing it was a vacation fling that ended at checkout time. He had a blossoming career while I was trying to salvage mine. Romance just did not fit into our busy lives.

"We'll always have Caye Caulker," I said in my best Bogart impression.

That made him smile. We'd spent a few nights curled around in other in bed after sex, his head on my chest. I recalled one special night when we watched *Casablanca* as the tropical winds tickled our overheated skin. Perfect. Then, I let him go. And go he did, with a few glances over his shoulder until he was out of the door and out of my life. It sucked. I felt as if a hole the size of a manhole cover had been gouged out of my chest.

I walked out onto the patio and stayed there until I was sure he was gone. Only then did I call Fi to let her know I was heading home. Alone. Just as I had left.

"OKAY, JACK, LET'S HIT THE SCALE BEFORE WE HIT THE ice," Bjorn said as soon as I entered the locker room. "You can't out-train a bad diet."

I'd heard that for the past four weeks. And it was true. No denying it. I'd come back from Caye feeling glum over the loss of another lover, but something Fiona had said on the ride home from the airport had wiggled through the gloom like a sliver of sun cuts through the rain clouds.

"You're looking at things wrong, Jack. Instead of focusing on leaving him, look at how fucking amazing it was to be with him and that you, Jack O'Leary, had a younger lover who lavished attention on you and was well-pleased in bed and out. Also, I love your snapshots of you and him. Can I *please* send a dozen to your ex?"

"No!"

"You don't let me have any fun!"

Still, Fi was right. I had managed to find and please a gorgeous man ten years my junior. That was something to feel good about. My ego began to grow slowly. Knowing I could still please a lover made me feel better about myself. And that had started to leak into my hockey life. Which was why I settled on signing up with Bjorn Persson, a personal trainer at his facility in Falmouth, Massachusetts. The man was legendary. He'd worked with many of the pros, including several from the Boston Rebels. The four-week training camp was intense. I do not know how I survived the first day. I barely made it to the ice for day two, but I did. And then I showed for days three, four, five, etc., and the training got easier. Not easy. Bjorn did not do *easy*. But easier.

Coming into the final week, I was down ten pounds, my speed had increased, my focus on basic mechanics had improved, and my endurance had risen.

The Railers were about to get a brand-new captain when preseason began next week. All thanks to two magical weeks with Tian. If I ever saw that man again, I would kiss him for the bolster he had given my sagging ego. I'd also kiss him because I missed his laughter and sunny disposition. We could have been good, I think, if life hadn't pulled us apart.

"If I maintain weight, do I get to have a banana split after sprints?" I asked, stepping up onto the scale in front of ten other elite players, all younger than I was, and all just as hungry. The guys chuckled.

"No, but you can join the others for another hour in the weight room followed by fruit smoothies on the quad," Bjorn replied.

"That's not as inspiring as you seem to think," I countered and got a short huff of a laugh from the towering Swedish ex-Olympian.

The fruit smoothie, an hour later, tasted mighty fine. As did the knowledge I'd bench-pressed more than any of the hotshot youngsters. Yep, that smoothie tasted *damn* fine.

"CAP, DO YOU THINK THAT THE RAILERS WILL EVER again have a streak like we had in the Rowe-Madsen days?"

I scrubbed at my beard, neatly trimmed but still on my face. I couldn't bring myself to shave it off, as Tian had loved it so much. Not that I had anyone to take his place in my bed. I doubted anyone could, but keeping the whiskers reminded me of our short but incredible time together. And that always made me feel better about myself. I stroked my chin as I contemplated the question from one of about fifteen reporters gathered around me on the first day of training camp.

"Well, Issac, I think that we're going to see a new team this year, filled with great talent. We have some great rookies this year who will be trying to make the roster. Did you see our representation at this year's rookie camps?"

Issac, a reporter from a local sports blog and a pretty decent guy, nodded. "I did, and while those kids are in the pipeline, we're going to need more from the veterans."

"Agreed," I said, and got head bobs from the press at my cubicle. "I know that I'm coming into this season lighter, stronger, and with a fire in my heart that I hope to spread to the rest of the team. I know Gunny over there," I jerked my hairy chin at Noah Gunnarsson holding court in the corner, "has been working hard all summer, just like Trick. We're all hunkering down to bring this city a winning team. I think you'll be pleased at what you see during our first preseason game against Philly in a few weeks."

They fired a few more questions at me, then filed out when the press manager for the team told them to. Layton Foxx, newly appointed Senior Director of Public and Media Relations for the Railers, herded them to the press room where they could speak with the GM while we players were put through a day of testing.

I strolled through the locker room, stopping to talk with each man, asking how their summer went and how the partners and kids were doing. Gunny and his race car driver were stupidly happy; I could tell by the goofy grin on his face when he mentioned him. Trick was dating a retired football star and seemed happy as a clam. His attitude would be under my scrutiny this season. I knew love could do miraculous things for a man. Not that I loved Tian. I mean, that would be silly. I'd known him for two weeks. And sure, those were amazing weeks, but love was something you built together. Over time. And we were not together, nor would we ever be, as long as we were both professional athletes. But the point still remained.

Once I'd chatted with everyone, I stood in the center of the horseshoe-shaped room, careful not to step on the Railers logo in the center of the mat. We did not need any bad juju.

"Okay, men, I know you're all looking forward to a day filled with grueling tests both on and off the ice. Surely you all were training hard during the summer and are in peak physical condition, so nothing to worry about, right?" I asked and received a round of replies that seemed to be mostly upbeat.

"I love the VO2 test!" Gunny shouted and got pelted with socks.

"Yeah, we all love that one," I grunted as the men

moaned. "I know the trainers and coaches are about ready for us, but I wanted to take a few minutes to talk with you guys. I know last season was disappointing. Yeah, we made the playoffs, and that's something to be proud of. Getting shunted out in the first round was shit." The men murmured in agreement. "I feel that a lot of our trouble was here in the locker room. I was going through some personal stuff that pulled me down, and I wasn't here mentally to keep the locker room in the right frame of mind." They all started to coddle. "No, hey, no." I held up a hand. "I failed you all in that regard. It will *not* happen this season. I had a great summer, have moved into a new place, and am ready to devote myself to this game one hundred and ten percent."

They all grunted and clapped. "So, now the rest is up to you. Your captain is here, leaner and meaner and ready to knock fuckers off their skates. What are you baboons ready to do to bring the Cup to Harrisburg again?" Everyone shouted different things. Forwards wanted to score more, goalies be scored on less, and my fellow D-men wanted to knock fuckers off their skates. "Excellent! I love that grit! From this point forward, this team is all about cohesion. Working together as a unit. I want to see you bringing energy, toughness, and eagerness to every practice, every game, every time your skates touch ice. Together we can build something incredible. As a team that works as one, we can bring the Cup back to Harrisburg. Together we can build our own legacy!"

They all rose. Fists pumped the air. A dozen or so fell on me, slapping my back, ruffling my hair, and saying how proud they were to be Railers. That was the drive and passion we needed from the guys and from me on the daily. Last year, the shit with Paula had distracted me, pulled me down into a pit where I couldn't see one good thing about myself or my life. Now I was better, lighter, stronger, ready to take on the rest of the league. And so much of that new spirit was due to Tian. Someday, I would thank him for those magical two weeks. He'd been the keystone of my slow climb out of misery and self-doubt. As my team filed out to conduct their testing and get the new season underway, I whispered a heartfelt thanks. Not to any saint. No, I offered up a tender gratitude to Tian and the joy he had brought into my life. I sent it off with a kiss of my mother's gold cross that hung around my neck. Wherever he was and whatever he was doing, I hoped he felt a gentle caress of affection and warmth and knew it was from me.

EIGHT

Tian

SEPTEMBER MEANT MAMMOTH LAKES. DRYLAND training, mornings when sweat slicked down my spine, my breath burned in the thin mountain air, and resistance bands bit into my shoulders until every muscle screamed. Afternoons at the airbag, throwing myself off ramps until my body was bruised from endless switch backside 900s, frontside 1080 attempts, and half-spun 1620 setups. My thighs burned, shoulders ached from hauling myself upright after each slam into the airbag, and my lungs felt like they were lined with fire, but I kept climbing back up, forcing every muscle to remember what perfection had to feel like. and my brain overloaded with spin counts and grab tweaks. The mountains we loved weren't snow-covered yet, but the practice airbag gave me the chance to test tricks, land them safely, and keep building toward something that would set me apart from the rest. Something the selection committee couldn't ignore when the Olympic trials came.

I was working my way up to a monster of a Big Air trick. Separate pieces drilled over and over—the approach, the takeoff, the spin initiation, the grab, the landing mechanics—all had to be perfect on their own before I could stitch them together into the full run. If I could lock it down in time for the World Cup in Europe and nail it there, my name would be hung on the Olympic selection committee's wall as a solid option. Back it up with strong finishes in the Grand Prix and the Dew Tour, and I'd be a shoo-in. That was the ladder in my head every time I hit the airbag.

"Man, I can't wait until there's actual snow again," Derek, one of the guys I trained with, muttered as we trudged back up the stairs to reset. He was my age; we'd been riding the same circuits for years. "Dryland's good and all, but nothing beats the real thing."

"Yeah, can't argue with that," I said, shifting my board under my arm. "Snow's the whole point."

He grinned, but it didn't quite reach his eyes. "Guess I'm not pushing as hard this season. Married life, you know?" He paused as we joined the short queue. "Jenna's pregnant."

"Jeez, man, congrats," I said warmly, meaning it.

I pulled him into a one-armed bro-hug, grinning because Derek had always been head-over-heels for

Jenna and seeing him so happy made me happy too. He deserved this, the family he'd dreamed about, and I couldn't help but feel a surge of pride for him. He'd always been a solid rider and a better friend. He was also the only one I'd told—well, in a loose way—about what had happened on the cay, and only because he'd pushed me to trade stories about our breaks. Him? Having a pool installed at his house in Aspen. Me? Well, sun, sea, and sex. It had made him laugh and shake his head, and it had felt good to share even a sliver of that with someone who knew me.

Dishonest after I'd realized how much the two weeks had meant to me, yeah, but hey, I'd told someone.

"Thinking maybe I'll back off after this season," Derek admitted. "Be a good dad, not get myself killed on a trick, be a good husband."

"You'll miss it, man," I pointed out.

"Maybe I'll manage, or work with a sponsor, get some weekend-level tricks in on my downtime, but yeah... I'm thinking about it. Got a call from a big sponsor and I'm not sure I want to commit."

"What about the O-team?" I asked with caution. Both of us wanted a spot on the Olympic squad, had been working our way to it for a long time, and now he was backing off.

"Family means more right now," he said, and he smiled so widely I couldn't argue with what he believed.

I clapped a hand on his shoulder, said all the right things, but inside was a different matter.

That was what happened when you got involved with someone. You lost focus. You softened. I couldn't afford that. Not now, not ever. Not me. I was going all the way. I'd made the right choice even if Jack was in my thoughts more times than he should be.

Every practice run felt as if it mattered—the slam of my body into the airbag reverberating through my bones, the hiss of compressed air rushing around me. Abel Riding—a former X Games legend turned trainer —and my coach yelled through the chaos with sharp, unmistakable commands: "Tuck sooner! Spot your landing earlier! Hold that grab!" Other coaches chimed in, their shouts mixing with the dull thud of boards hitting plastic, until it felt like the whole mountain was conspiring to push us riders harder.

Every twist, every off-axis grab, every stomp on the inflated surface was one step closer to proving I belonged on the biggest stage. He barked corrections at me, and the other coaches had plenty to say as well. Younger riders watched with wide eyes, and a couple of my peers—Derek included—muttered about me trying things they weren't ready to risk. But risk was the point. My breakout year had brought the sponsors circling, and now I had to show them it wasn't a fluke.

The truth was, I should have been buzzing with adrenaline and focus. And I was, mostly. But every time

I hiked back up the stairs to reset, I caught myself thinking about Jack. The press of his mouth, the rasp of his beard, the sound of his voice when he told me it was okay. It had been weeks since Caye Caulker, but he was still in my head more than I'd ever admit. I kept telling myself I was right not to chase it. My schedule was jammed, my life measured in rotations and competitions, and I didn't have room for distractions. Even ones with blue eyes and broad shoulders.

By the time I crashed back in my condo every night, my muscles ached in that way that meant I'd worked hard, but I was buzzing and high on life. Even more so tonight because the hockey preseason had started and there were games streaming. My thumb hovered over the options. My team faced Carolina in what promised to be a physical, intense battle. But instead, I ignored the New York game and cued up Railers versus Boston. That told me everything I didn't want to say out loud. In pre-season, not all the big names played—I wasn't even sure Jack would be on the ice, but fuck, there he was, as the camera followed them through the tunnel and heading onto the ice, leading his team.

The camera zoomed in on his face, sweat dampening the ginger-blond beard still clinging to his jaw. God, that beard. He was strong, carved from stone, blue eyes blazing with intensity. Gorgeous. So sexy, I could feel the heat spike in my blood just staring at the TV. He radiated command, and I couldn't tear my eyes off him.

Jack looked sharp. Leaner, faster, more alive than he had been on the flight to Belize. His focus was absolute, every shift a statement. I felt something twist in my chest—pride, maybe. And longing. Damn it, I missed him.

Midway through the second, Boston's winger broke free on a rush, but Jack read the play as though he'd scripted it himself. He pivoted, angled his body perfectly, and cut the guy off with a textbook hip-check that had the commentators shouting his name. The puck squirted loose, and seconds later, he threaded a crisp pass that set up the Railers' rush the other way. Goal! When Boston pressed again on the power play, Jack dropped to the ice to block a rocket of a shot, popping back up without missing a beat, directing traffic in front of his goalie like a general. He looked every inch the captain, fire in his stride, and it made my chest ache with pride.

The Railers scored again, late in the second. Jack threw himself into every check, every block, and when the buzzer sounded and they'd won two to nothing, I caught myself smiling at the screen like an idiot.

Rinkside, a reporter intercepted Jack as he came off the ice. "Captain O'Leary," she called, shoving a mic under his chin, "what changed over the summer? You look sharper, faster, more focused than ever." Jack's gaze slid past the scrum of cameras for the briefest second, something unspoken flickering in his eyes, before he answered in that calm, dry tone of his.

"Sometimes you just need to get away, clear your head, remember what makes this game matter. I had two weeks that reminded me who I was. That's all." Everyone else nodded, as if it were about conditioning or coaching. But me? I instinctively knew it was about the cay.

I should message him.

Hell, I even picked up my phone, thumb hovering over Jack's name. We'd swapped numbers on the cay just to coordinate dinners and dive times, never once saying we'd use them once the trip was over. But now? I wanted to send him something—just a quick *well done, you were incredible out there*. Would that be breaking our pact, shattering the line we'd drawn around fourteen days of sun, sex, and then goodbye? I stared down at some of the casual shots I'd taken when he hadn't seen me—we hadn't gone the selfie route often, but when I'd had a chance, I captured an image or two. One was him on the balcony, shirt off, the late sun painting his skin gold while he leaned on the railing and stared out to sea, a beer bottle dangling from his fingers. He'd looked so peaceful, so solid, and seeing the photo now made my chest tight. The other was taken in bed, his head tipped back in laughter at something dumb I'd said, his beard shadowing his jaw, teeth flashing white, eyes alive. That one gutted me the most, because it wasn't just sexy, it was happy—and I wanted to be the reason he laughed like that again.

The vibration from my phone broke the spell. My agent's name lit up the display. I thumbed it on.

"MarvTech wants to talk," she said without preamble—that was how Marissa Logan worked. "Big deal, Tian. Not quite Red Bull numbers, but close. We'll set a meeting this week."

Big money. Bigger exposure. Everything I'd been working toward since I strapped onto a board. My sponsors wanted more, the media wanted more, and I was ready to give it to them. So why did part of me wish I could trade it all for another night tangled up with Jack O'Leary?

NOVEMBER UNDER THE FLOODLIGHTS, CRISP ALPINE AIR sharp in my lungs, the roar of the crowd like a living wall pressing in. Flags whipped in the cold night wind, boards scraped against the icy start ramp with a harsh, metallic bite, and the floodlights turned every snowflake into glittering diamond dust. Cameras panned to each of us at the top, mist puffing from our mouths as we psyched ourselves up. World Cup events in Europe were insane, but Austria in particular was another level. The landing zone was carved out of glacier ice, with music thundering from the speakers; the crowd was packed in, as if it were already the Olympic Games.

I tugged my gloves tighter, board edge biting into the start ramp. The US guys had already put down some solid runs, but I was hungry for more than solid. The announcer called my name—Tian-Lei Cai-Wilder, USA!—and the roar from the crowd shook the air.

I dropped in for my first run; muscles coiled and threw a switch backside 1440 melon. Clean, high amplitude, stomped it like I'd done a thousand times into the airbag.

When the score came up—84.5, good enough for provisional second—Abel barked, "Good start."

I nodded, already knowing it wasn't enough to win, but it was the banker I needed.

On my second run, I went bigger, doing a frontside 1800 mute with five full rotations, the board locked in my grip like it was glued there. I felt the wobble as soon as I landed, board chatter rattling up my legs, my hand brushing the snow.

"Fuck," I snarled as I stopped near Abel.

He shook his head and mouthed, "It's okay."

The score flashed 79.0. Strong, but not perfect, and shit, it dropped me behind the Swiss rider, Silvan Roth, always my biggest rival.

By the time I dropped in for my third run, my lungs were heaving, legs trembling from the strain of the night, gloves tightening on the board edge as if I could squeeze more strength into them. My heart hammered like a drum; the weight of the crowd, the lights, and my own expectations pressed down on me. I knew this was it—one last chance to put everything on the line, one run to prove I belonged among the very best, one shot that could change my future. Backside 1620 indy to tail —two grabs in one spin, super technical. I launched off the lip, everything clicking into place. The pop was massive, the air felt endless, and I spotted the landing from a mile up. My legs absorbed the shock like steel springs; my arms shot skyward, the landing clean and smooth. The crowd erupted, my teammates pounding the boards on the fence. Score: 91.2. Silver medal position.

I ripped my helmet off, grinning so wide it hurt, snow clinging to my hair. Cameras caught everything, and I lifted my arm high, waving like always. My parents were watching from the hotel, because even though they came to Austria every year to see me compete, Mom refused to spectate at the landing zone; she couldn't handle it in person. From sleeping on friends' floors and in shitty hostels to now staying in first-class luxury courtesy of MarvTech, they'd been there for every step, my biggest support system, and I wanted them to see me now, riding higher than ever.

And Jack.

Abel's hands landed heavy on my shoulders, his voice rough with pride. "That's it, kid. That's your name on the Olympic potentials list for sure."

I whooped; there was no feeling like it.

But this time I was waving at Jack, even if he wasn't there. Just in case—would he have seen this? Was it even streamed back in the States, up in PA? Was he even interested? I wanted to hug him, I wanted him to see how well I'd done, I wanted him to be proud of me. What the hell was wrong with me? The thought tangled in my chest, fierce and raw, as the cheers washed over me.

What mattered more—standing here on the podium with silver glinting in the floodlights, or the impossible wish of Jack O'Leary looking at me with pride in his eyes?

I couldn't decide.

NINE

Jack
_____

"YOU START ON THE ORNAMENTS AND I'LL—" I PAUSED with the end of one silver garland strand in my hand. "Fi, don't argue with me about this anymore. It's January 1st. The tree has to go. It's shedding and I have a road trip into Canada that'll keep me away from home for two weeks."

"I'll water it," she said, crossing her arms over her chest, then setting her chin. She could be really defiant at times. Most of the time, to be honest.

"You're leaving for the UK tomorrow, then off to Moldova, and then a stop in Berlin. When do you think you can water it?" I waved a hand at the fat green spruce that was growing browner and thinner by the day.

"When I get home."

"I'll be back before you will." Her lips flattened. "It

has to go. The holidays are over. I appreciated you buying it, decorating it, and naming it Steve so it would feel more at home here, but the time has come. All good things must come to an end."

My thoughts pulled up an image of Tian spread over the hotel bed, nude, breathtakingly beautiful, beckoning me to join him. I still missed him. Smoky memories of slick skin, strong questing fingers, and soft laughs haunted my nights. Maybe haunted wasn't the right word. They lingered in my dreams, teasing me to wakefulness with a craving in my chest and a hard dick. That good thing had ended. And now Steve the Spruce had to hit the curb.

"I wish you'd leave it up just a little longer." She pouted the prettiest pout ever to be pouted.

I tugged the garland off with a jerk that made a tiny bell on a glass angel ornament ring out.

Her pout morphed into a gasp. "Mom always left it up until January seventh until after the Feast of the Epiphany."

"That's not fair."

She shrugged. "Maybe not but if you take the tree and decorations down before the sixth it brings bad luck. And we do not want any evil vibes to settle on you."

Okay yes, that was true. This season had been freaking phenomenal. We were solidly in first place in our division, every line was clicking, and everyone was pumped. On a personal note, I was having the best season of my long career. I had twenty-one goals and sixteen assists already, which compared to Gunny and Trick, and a few other hotshot scorers was not huge but for a defenseman midway through the season? I'd take it any time. My TOI was high, my plus/minus was plus thirty-two and my hits were climbing to plus sixty. Penalty minutes were low, blocked shots were high. I'd never played better.

"Fine, we'll leave it up." She smiled so sweetly it gave me a cavity just looking at her. "Do you always win every debate we have?"

"Yes." She skipped over, ponytail bouncing, to hug me tight. A vanilla floral scent engulfed me as she nestled into my chest, cheek over my heart. "I love you."

"Mm-hmm." I rested my hairy chin atop her head as the tree dropped a dozen needles in spite. "Love you too."

"I know. Did you see that Tian—"

"Fi, that's off limits," I reminded her gently. I'd never disclosed that I checked in on him on Instagram and Tik Tok when I had a moment to relax and drift off into recollections.

She tipped her head up to stare at me. "I think you should text him. Just let him know that you're—"

"Nope." I kissed her nose then wiggled free of the

hug. "Now, since we're not taking down the tree…" My phone buzzed in my back pocket. "One second."

She sighed but went over to pet Steve. A dozen plus needles hit the hardwood floors and she glanced over her shoulder wearing a chagrined expression before dashing off to *hopefully* find the broom. Such a brat.

I checked the incoming call and saw it was from Gunny. A call from a kid? Must be serious. I tapped the green button, and his face came into view in a small screen on the bottom left.

"Gunny, what's up?" I asked right off. I could tell by just looking at the guy that he was stressed out. He blew at a blond curl dangling into his eye. He'd decided to not cut his hair this season because he was currently tied with Trick for goals. Hockey players could be superstitious in the extreme. We'd not get into some of the crazy shit I'd seen over the years. "You sick?"

We had a big game against Carolina tomorrow at home.

"No, I just read the morning hockey news report in *Ice Beat in the 'Burg*."

I walked over to my patio to gaze out at the snow on the little picnic table and two chairs now covered with plastic.

"Did you see the rumors out of Detroit?"

I hadn't. I did my best to not get into online sports sites. Most were just armchair dudes speculating over this or that and with the trade deadline coming in two months tittle-tattle or outright lies were going to fire up. Also, I didn't care what the press thought about me. I was doing the best I could do, and if the coach and GM were happy then to hell with what some Chad or Brad with a podcast set up in their living room thought.

"Gunny, there's no reason to get fired up over anything said on *Ice Beat*. I know Preston Mills likes to think he has a finger on the pulse of the league but he's just a dude with his nose in the dirt."

"No, I mean… yeah, I know he can be a shit at times but he's saying that the Railers are looking to bring him in to bolster the second line forward situation. Cap, I cannot play on the same team as that dick."

"Okay, slow your roll a bit kid," I said firmly. Gunny blew out a breath. "What dick are we even talking about? I know about eighty in the league."

"Jari Lankinen."

Oh. Oh. Now that was a name I knew well. The last name anyway. Anyone who lived in this town or played on this team was well aware of the devastating head injury Tennant Rowe-Madsen had suffered years ago at the hands of Aarni Lankinen, Jari's father.

"It's probably just a rumor, Gunny. You know Preston likes to toss out stupid headlines just to get people to click or call in to his podcast. I'd not put much stock into it."

"Can you look into it, Cap? My dads and Tennant are super close. Pop's already saying that if the Railers allow a Lankinen to wear the dusky blue he will call the people he knows."

Jesus. Stan. I loved the guy, everyone did, and he was HHOF goalie royalty, but he did have a tendency to go off like a rocket.

"Yeah, sure, I'll poke around and see if I can sniff anything concrete up. But you know if the team is dealing quietly behind the scenes no one will say a thing to me or anyone else until the contracts are signed. Tell Stan to chill out and go watch an Elvis movie. And you also need to shake it off, the kid. Even if they were to bring this Jari in, there's nothing you could do about it. We don't have to like all of our teammates, but we do have to play our game at maximum no matter who we're passing a puck to, right?" He didn't reply. "Right, Gunny?"

"Yeah, right, Cap." He didn't sound convinced.

"Okay, see you at morning skate. Stay off social media and I'll see what I can dig up. It'll probably just be some clickbait shit, and we'll keep kicking ass and chewing bubble gum," I reassured the young man as best I could. Stupid podcasters.

I was pulling my coat on when Coach entered the locker room. He looked tired but not tight.

"Jack, before you go, I have some good news," he

opened with, smiling at Gunny, who smiled politely back.

"Good news today would be welcomed," I said, then glanced down to button my winter coat.

"Agreed. The GM has just gotten word from USA Hockey that you've been chosen to represent America in the Olympics next month in Italy. Congratulations."

I stood there like a dolt, fingers locked on brass buttons, staring at the hand my head coach was shoving at me. Gunny hooted.

"I… but Trick and Gunny are the young ones," I stammered.

"Well, it seems they wanted some vets on their team, and with your tenure in the league and the outstanding season you're having they would like to have you wear the red, white, and blue."

"No shit?" I asked, coat still unbuttoned.

Coach chuckled. "No shit. My hand is getting tired of hanging here in space."

I hurried to clasp it and shake it hard. "Thanks, Coach, this is a real honor. I'm just… so old."

"With age comes wisdom," Coach said, then shifted his attention to Gunny. "Congratulations again, Jack. Well deserved. Make sure you take sunscreen for the snow glare."

Sunscreen. Right. I'd not laid eyes on my bottle of sunscreen since I'd tossed it under the sink on my return from Caye Caulker. My heart skipped a beat as I recalled smearing thick white lotion on Tian's warm skin. Tian. Holy hell. Had he made the team? Would we see each other there? What would I say if we ran into each other? Would it be horribly awkward? Would we talk, or share a beer, or pick up where we'd left off in the Caribbean?

Only time would tell...

I KNEW THAT THE US TEAM NEEDED PROMO PHOTOS.

Didn't mean I had to like having them taken.

"Okay, Jack, if you could turn this way and lift your chin. Hmm, Louisa, can we do something about the wild hairs of that beard. Oh, and please give him more concealer under his eyes. I've wheeled bags through customs that were smaller."

I shot a look at Pete Starinski, or Starry as he was known in Florida. "Did that picture-taker just call me old?"

Starry, another defenseman, chuckled. "I think so. Do we want to slap him upside the head with these pretty red, white, and blue sticks?

"Let me think about it," I replied as Louisa, a lovely woman corralling us idiot hockey players, arrived to touch up the bags under my eyes.

This patriotic imagery was nice; don't get me wrong, but what I wanted most right now was, in order of importance, to get to Italy, find Tian, kiss him, and fall asleep. If the kissing led to other things in the privacy of a hotel room, then sleep would naturally have to be put off. Personally, I'd have been happy to skip all of this. Not that I wasn't proud to play for my country but being draped in the flag and told to pretend I was thinking deep thoughts was not Jack O'Leary.

It was too much hoopla. I just wanted to get over to Europe, play hockey, and beat Canada. That was half of the conversation among the top players from America on the flight over. That was the Holy Grail for us, and it wasn't easy to accomplish. But we had fantastic players and coaches. We had a solid chance. I'd give it my all. This was my first and for sure last time I would ever be invited. I wanted to go out big. Retirement was a year away now and what better way to clock out than with a gold medal, a Cup win, and Tian in my life. Somehow. Somehow, we would make it work. *If* he was interested in making it work.

"His beard is too wooly," Louisa announced to the room.

The photographer, some wiry guy with a bowl cut hairdo and thick glasses, stormed over to me.

"Mr. Hockey Player, your facial hair is being contrary. Please shave."

"Yeah, nope." I stared down at the pencil-thin man in the black shawl and matching leggings. "Not going to happen. Just pluck a few."

"How can I do my job when these idiots don't listen," he huffed then set Louisa to tugging out wild red hairs with her little silver tweezers. The other guys in the room were in hysterics.

I'd give the press a lot of leeway, but I wasn't shaving my beard. Tian had loved running his fingers through it and that meant it was staying. At least until we had a chance to meet up and talk in Italy. Then, if he had someone else in his life—something against which I prayed every other day—I'd shave it. Maybe. Maybe not. It was a lucky beard now. Maybe this wild, thick ginger mass would sit on my face until they planted me in the cold green hills outside Dublin next to some of my distant relatives.

"Seems you would have better control of your beard," Starry teased an hour later when we were all finally done being plucked, contoured, and photographed.

"They have a mind of their own," I tossed over my shoulder, Starry at my side. We D-men tended to hang together like a troop of monkeys. I was ready to go home and finish packing, counting down the days until I could see Tian again. We'd been given a nearly three-week break to participate on the US team, and I planned to make the most of it. I'd never been to Italy. I'd had daydreams of shady coffees in romantic little cafes with Tian tucked into my side.

Winning gold and seeing Tian.

TEN

Tian
_____

I WAS AT THE FINAL QUALIFIER AT THE US GRAND PRIX at Mammoth Mountain. I was there, sore from the last brutal practice runs, every joint aching from repetition, but ready to put it all on the line. This was the one—secure a medal here, and my place on the Olympic team was locked. I was already all but in, but just one more podium would seal it. I could feel the weight of the season behind me, a trophy rack of medals from every stop so far, proof that I hadn't just had a breakout year—I'd sustained it.

I was sprawled on the couch with ice packs on my knees when the alert buzzed through my sports app. I'd added the Railers to my New York feed weeks ago, telling myself it was just to keep tabs on the competition, not for any other reason. The roster announcements for Team USA hockey were coming out in drips and fragments, and I thumbed the notification open without much thought. Then I saw it—front and center, Jack O'Leary. My chest tightened. He was going to Italy. He was going to the Olympics.

And I'd probably be joining him—and the thought made my stomach lurch. Pride, excitement, and raw nerves all tangled together. The Olympics had been the dream since I'd first strapped into a board, but now it wasn't just about medals and sponsors. It meant being in the same place as Jack again, and I couldn't decide if that possibility thrilled me, terrified me, or both at once. The thought of seeing him again—being forced into the same orbit because we were both Team USA—made my chest tighten. Maybe I'd get the chance to talk to him, maybe even undo the whole once-and-done thing we'd sworn to on the cay. Did he even want that? Did I? I was the best I'd ever been, standing at the peak of my career, and yet the idea of Jack looking at me, of him being proud of me, pulled at me as much as any medal ever could.

My cell buzzed with a reminder I was scheduled at a MarvTech meet and greet. I shuffled into the bathroom, stretching out cold muscles, feeling new aches where I'd taken a stupidly bad tumble on loose powder. Rookie mistake.

A call came in from my parents as I brushed my teeth, and I spat out the paste. I might need to be downstairs by ten, but I'd never miss a call with my mom and dad. Fuck the rest of the world.

"Morning, sweetheart!" Mom chimed, her voice bright and warm.

"Morning! How's the room?" I'd set this up for them, the best view of the mountain and the halfpipe, a suite at the Mammoth Mountain Inn overlooking the competition runs. They were thrilled with it, sending me photos of the fireplace and the balcony view last night, even though I knew Mom wouldn't be standing there watching when it was her baby descending at nearly forty mph, with the kind of trick that made her cover her eyes every time.

"A huge bed, Tian. Beautiful!"

"Big bed, but your mom stole all the covers last night," Dad grumbled, his voice echoing.

"I did not!" Mom shot back, laughter bubbling under her words. "You hog the bed like a bear!"

They were so loved up it was ridiculous, laughing over each other before both yelled at once, "Good luck for today, Tian!"

"Bye!" Dad added, and I could picture him ambling away to stare out at the view — always liked his alone time, which left Mom and me.

Her voice became hushed, worried. "I saw that tumble on social media—are you okay?"

"I'm fine, Mom," I said with a laugh. "Nothing to worry about."

The truth was the fall had spooked me more than I wanted to admit. Still, I wasn't about to let them hear the crack in my certainty. Not when they were this excited for me and when I needed every bit of confidence I could find.

By the time my sponsor stuff was done, and I was ready for my first run, the crowd was buzzing, snow guns blasting fine mist into the crisp air, coaches pacing like caged animals. My board was waxed, my body strung tight with nerves and anticipation. One more run, one more medal, and I'd be boarding a plane to Italy with Team USA.

For me and the other US riders, this wasn't just about chasing FIS points and World Cup medals—it was about the added pressure of US team selection hanging over every run. International rivals like Silvan Roth from Switzerland or the Japanese prodigies viewed Mammoth as just another stop on the World Cup circuit, another chance to climb the standings. For us, a missed podium could mean missing the Olympic team altogether. That tension made every final electric. I only needed to get silver to clinch an Olympic berth.

Only.

Famous last words.

Silvan caught me at the top of the run, grinning like the cocky bastard he was. "Hope you're ready to eat Swiss snow, Tian," he teased, bumping his fist against mine.

"Yeah, yeah. Don't get too comfortable up there," I shot back, trying to sound casual even though my stomach was a knot of nerves.

Then Abel was in my ear, gripping my shoulders, voice low but sharp. "Keep it level, Tian. Nothing so fancy you crash out. You've got this if you stay clean. Focus." He gave me a little shake, eyes burning into mine. "One last solid run and you're in."

Then it was my time. The world narrowed to the ramp, the wind, and the thud of my heartbeat. My runs were a blur of muscle and instinct, each landing punching through my legs, each cheer rolling over me like surf. When the points were tallied, Silvan edged me out for first, but my name was right under his.

Silver.

Abel grabbed me hard, nearly shaking me off my feet, his grin wild. "Yes!"

I was going to Italy.

I'm going to have a reason to see Jack.

That night, my parents insisted on taking me out to celebrate, and somehow we ended up at a long table in the hotel restaurant with Silvan and another man who wandered over to say hello. Mom, of course, encouraged them to sit with us. Silvan clapped me on the shoulder, then gestured proudly. "This is Lukas Vogel, my partner."

"Lovely to meet you," Mom said brightly. "How did you two meet?"

Lukas smiled, a little shy. "I'm a dentist back in Zurich. We met through friends, and, well… we never really stopped talking after that first dinner."

I sat there thinking, How do they make that work? He was traveling the circuit all winter, and Lukas anchored in Switzerland with a job that didn't exactly scream flexibility. Yet seeing them together—Silvan's hand finding Lukas's under the table, Lukas leaning in close to laugh at some story Dad told—they made it seem effortless. My parents were charmed, conversation flowed, and before long, everyone was trading stories and laughing.

Eventually, Mom and Dad excused themselves, hugging me before leaving for their room. Lukas rose as well, brushing a kiss over Silvan's lips. "I'll be up in ten," Silvan murmured back, his smile soft. When Lukas had gone, Silvan turned to me.

"You seem quiet tonight, my friend. What's wrong?"

"Nothing." Jealousy over Silvan and Lukas? Loneliness when I'd realized what it was like to be with someone?

"Bull crap," Silvan snorted. "You just clinched your Olympic spot. We get to do this all again in Italy, and you can't crack a smile."

"Nothing's wrong," I repeated, forcing a smile. "Just… thinking about…"

"About how a devastatingly handsome Swiss man stole your gold?"

"Asshole," I snarked, and then sat back in my chair. "Your Lukas is a nice guy."

"My lover is everything," Silvan admitted and leaned on his elbows. "And I love him more than what we do."

I fake-clasped my chest. "More than Big Air?"

"Every day."

"How does it work, him in Switzerland, you on the road?"

Silvan waggled his eyebrows, "Naked Facetime is a thing."

I groaned. "I did not need to know that."

Silvan grinned knowingly. "You're wound too tight. Love is love, my friend. We make it work across an ocean, across crazy schedules. I knew after one date, before we'd even stopped talking, that he was it for me."

I tried to laugh it off, but his words landed like a rock in my chest.

After one date, he knew?

Remind me again why Jack and I decided on a vacation fling?

How did I even agree to stay away from Jack and pretend the two weeks were nothing to me when I'd already started to fall for him?

Getting to Italy would be a whole production. Team USA would fly us out together, a plane packed with athletes from every discipline—snowboarders, skiers, figure skaters, even the speedskating crew.

But no hockey players.

They were still playing their season and would land at the last freaking minute. I knew exactly when they'd be flying out and had marked it in my online calendar.

I was excited to see Jack and ask him if he might want to do more than hook up again, but also to talk and laugh and explore what had happened.

I was nervous as well. Scared he'd tell me he met someone in the meantime. Afraid it was just me that needed more of the connection we'd had.

The plane itself felt like a flying locker room—rows filled with athletes in hoodies and beanies, gear bags crammed into every overhead bin, the air thick with nerves and excitement. Some of us traded playlists, others passed snacks around, a few knocked out cold with noise-canceling headphones and neck pillows before we even left the runway. I sat there sore but wired, staring out at the ocean miles below, the hum of engines mixing with bursts of laughter and chatter as the hours dragged by. It was a long haul across the Atlantic, but we were heading to the Olympics, and the buzz never quieted.

I was sitting with a young guy who could talk more than me and was super affectionate. After jawing for two hours, Brett Mitchener wore himself out, like a toddler who'd run too hard at recess, and slumped against me. I didn't mind talking Big Air, I didn't mind him sleeping on me, but I *really* liked the quiet. The kid wasn't a medal hope going in, but he'd qualified, and hell, the Olympics weren't over until it was over, and I had a lot to do to keep ahead of these younger guys coming up.

Even if Brett was only six years younger than me.

Once we landed, the US Olympic Committee had us booked into one of the official athlete hotels, part of a cluster reserved for Team USA, with security at the doors and banners draped from the balconies. We'd all be together—rooming two to a suite—I was with Brett —eating in the giant cafeteria alongside other American athletes, living in that bubble of red, white, and blue. It was efficient, communal, and I knew that meant I'd be bumping into Jack at times. Just the thought of seeing him across the dining hall, or on the bus to the venues, had my pulse racing before I'd even packed a bag, and it was worse now I was here.

Today was the day the hockey guys arrived, and I wasn't lurking in reception, no matter what it looked like. I just happened to be there, that was all. As did Brett, who was leaning against me on the sofa, chatting about everything and nothing, elbowing me when he thought I wasn't paying attention, which was a lot. He always seemed to end up draped over me like a little brother who hadn't learned about personal space yet. And hell, I kind of liked the affection—he was harmless enough, all wide eyes and endless chatter about the halfpipe. His weight pressed into my shoulder as the sliding doors opened and the first players walked through, and my stomach dropped even though I told myself it was a coincidence I was sitting there. I stood, Brett falling away, then bouncing up on his toes and clinging to me like a limpet. He grinned at the new arrivals.

"Ooh, hockey players." He squeezed my arm as what I assumed were equipment managers for the team rolled in with sticks, hundreds of them, in protective bags. "I can tell by their sticks." He grinned up at me as I glanced down at him, and fuck, his idiot puppy face made me smile, because hell, I was in a good mood anyway.

I stared back at the players—and then I saw Jack. He was staring at me, but he wasn't smiling. His expression was fierce, tense, and fuck, this was not how I'd imagined seeing him again. I sent him a shy smile, and I got it wasn't right to go launch myself into his arms.

Only... He didn't smile back at me.

He stared at me with angry disdain, then turned away.

And if looks could kill?

I'd be dead.

ELEVEN

Jack

TIAN WAS RIGHT THERE.

Standing by a couch with some guy draped over him, and all I could picture was Tian's mouth on his, their bodies pressed together, my jealousy spiking hot and filthy, my brain painting them tangled up in bed and me locked out of it. My fists curled with the insane urge to smash something, jealousy roaring hotter than the jet lag. Something black and ugly welled up inside me as his gaze caught mine. Six goddamn months I'd been fooling myself, building castles in the sky about what we'd had, and for what? It had just been sex. Insanely hot sex, yeah, but nothing more, and I hated myself for believing it could have been. Any hope I'd clung to was ash in my mouth. We'd promised each other two weeks —sun, sea, and fucking—and nothing beyond that. Why the hell would he want me again? Of course, he'd find someone else. Someone his own age, someone easier. The pain stabbed like a shiv in my gut, sharp and merciless. I tore my gaze from him and stalked toward the reception desk, Starry still yammering about rooms with views and fuck knows what.

"Jack O'Leary," I barked at the young lady behind the desk. Her dark eyes flared. Starry elbowed me in the side. Hard. The jab in my ribs soothed the jealousy and pain throbbing in my breast. "Sorry, long flight. We're checking in. Jack O'Leary and Pete Starkinski."

He'd found someone else.

I meant nothing to him.

"Yes, sirs, tired is always happening," the desk clerk replied in English heavily accented with Italian.

Something kept prodding me to turn around. Look again. Maybe that was just some fan being overzealous. Cursing myself for my weakness, I glanced over my shoulder as Pete tried to talk up the reception desk gal as if she hadn't already dealt with loud Americans all day. I stared at the small fountain, two tall women in Olympic jackets chatting, and unbidden, my gaze fell on Tian. The asshole who had been hanging on him like a wet cape on a hook was sitting down. Tian's gaze was hot, and not in the I-want-your-body way but in the I-am-pissed-off way, which seemed unfair to me as he was the one with a blond bimbo feeling him up not ten seconds ago. He jerked his head to the left, then stamped off in that direction to slam through a door without even looking back to see if I was following him.

Fuck that. I was *not* going after him. He'd found another man. Some twinky shit who didn't have the manners to know not to be all PDA on him in public. Nope, I was not going after him. He made his twinky bed, let him lie in it.

"Can you get the key cards? I want to go check out the hotel pool," I said to Starry, then left him to deal with the check-in process. My carry-on was still in my hand. I chugged through the vast lobby, sidestepping luggage and athletes, then bulling through a door that led to what seemed to be meeting rooms. Nothing unusual in that. Hotels held conferences all the time. Probably we'd be in one later in the week to watch videos or hobnob with Olympic VIPs. I had no clue. Maybe we wouldn't enter one at all.

I paused as I tried to sniff out which way Tian had gone as if I were a damned bloodhound or something. To my right, a shape appeared, gave me a shove around a corner, and then planted his feet to block my escape.

"What the fuck was that?" Tian asked in a sharp but low growl.

"Get off me!"

"Are you too good to even say hello to me?"

Fuck, he looked sexy—his lips swollen and begging to be bitten, thighs taut in those jeans, every line of his lean body screaming to be touched—and it took everything in me not to slam him against the wall and grind into him right there. But I wouldn't let that derail my righteous anger. "Looked to me like you were too busy letting your new boyfriend climb all over you."

He blinked. "What?"

"I'm not doing this," I snapped, and pushed him away, using all my best moves to stop him from touching me, but he was wily and quick and back in front of me in a second.

"Seriously?" He snapped. "That's what this is all about? You're jealous?"

My temper flared even brighter. I was sick that I'd built anything in my head with him, and sick that I hadn't listened to my gut. I was older, stupid, and he was this young kid. Of course, he didn't want me.

"Fuck that. I am not jealous. I couldn't care less. What we had was just two weeks of fun and sun, right?"

He stepped back, his face suddenly blank. For a heartbeat, I thought I saw a flicker of shock, something raw and unguarded, but it disappeared in an instant, shuttered behind that fierce mask he was wearing so well right now. "Right. We fucked," he said in a dead tone. Then he stabbed me with a pointed finger, dead center in the US flag on my chest. "You want to forget it, fine, but at least have the decency to look at me!"

I was speechless. He thought I wanted to forget it. Was he bonkers?

"What? I don't want to—"

"Don't you dare dump your regrets about fucking me all over me now!" Tian shouted, his temper causing his cheeks to flush and his eyes to brighten with emotion. Lord, he was so beautiful, even prettier than I'd recalled. I fisted my hands to keep from reaching for him. Unsure now of how to reply, I sucked in a shaky breath and shook my head. "You have no reply? Nothing?" He seemed unbelieving, but he should know I was a man of few words. "What about you and that tall bastard that you were with when you exited the elevator?"

That snapped me out of my mental fog. "Starry's a teammate. Not that it matters."

"Brett is a teammate as well!"

"Yeah, but a little too fucking friendly," I snapped, the words ripping out of me before I could stop them. My temper was unleashed now. "Not that it matters because we mean nothing to each other, right?" I went for the jugular, and he hissed then stabbed a finger at me again. I caught it and gripped his hand hard, but he yanked it away.

"If you think that, then why are you yelling at me about my teammate?"

That about finished me off, and suddenly, all sense of what I was supposed to say flew out of the window. "I don't know!" I yelled in his face. "Maybe because I can't stop thinking about you, and that makes me edgy as fuck!"

His eyes flared. My fingers clenched tighter. The atmosphere in that tiny alcove shifted from red-hot anger to a foggy gray of uncertainty.

"Jack—"

"All I think about is you! Day and night. You've never left my mind since we left the cay behind. I dream about being inside you and wake up sweaty and sick with want. From the moment the coach told me I made the team, all I could think of was kissing you again and making love to you. And then when I first see you you're with some jerk, and I want you so much, so I didn't want to say anything because it hurt I wasn't enough for you to want me as well."

"Stop—"

I couldn't stop. The words kept pouring out, sharper and louder with every breath. "You'd obviously moved on!"

"I haven't moved on!" Tian shot back, his voice cracking under the strain.

"Well, how the hell would I know that? We promised radio silence, no texts, no calls, nothing!" My chest heaved, fury boiling over. "What did you expect me to think, huh?"

"I know what we said! I was there, Jack!" he shouted, eyes wild. "This is insane—why are we tearing each other apart in a fucking hallway?"

The door across the hall flew open, and an older woman in a sedate blue dress stalked up to us, her face pinched, the room behind her filled with people with papers in front of them. She then dressed us down in flowing Italian that neither of us understood, but we nodded along. Her gist was pretty clear. Shut the fuck up, you dumb, loud Americans, we're trying to have a meeting. With that dictate delivered, she stormed back into the conference room and slammed the door in our faces.

"Whoa shit," Tian whispered.

My temper subsided in an instant. "She should be a hockey coach," I muttered, my gaze refocusing on Tian. *My beautiful Tian.*

We were both breathing hard, as if we'd just gone twelve rounds in the ring, and all I could think about was dragging him somewhere dark and tearing into him again. The softer fantasies—anything more than raw sex—died in my throat, choking me, because I hated myself for wanting more when my body just screamed for him.

"I missed you," Tian confessed on a shaky breath, but what I really heard was the echo of all the nights I'd missed the sex, the heat, the way he made me lose control. But he sounded vulnerable. Sad. And the admission gutted me. It shredded any lingering envy, littering the bits on the wet tile floor under our shoes.

Now it was my turn.

"I missed you too, so damn much," I revealed, opening up as he had.

He moved like lightning, coming into my arms with a speed that shunted me back into wall with a grunt. His mouth crashed over mine, tongues colliding, teeth nipping, both of us rough and desperate, needing each other's bodies more than breath. I cupped his ass and moaned at the familiar feel of his body tight to mine. I slid my tongue into his mouth, licked and sucked, nipped at his lower lip, then kissed the place where I had tugged. He held my face, fingers carded into my beard, his mouth just as hungry and hot as I remembered. "Tian…"

"Jack, shit. Shit," he panted, as we ravaged each other's mouths. "Jack, my foot… ice… floor… missed this." My hip impacted a laundry cart, sending stacked towels to the tiles. I rubbed my teeth down along the side of his throat. "Jack, we can't… we can't do this here."

"Sure, we can," I growled across his thumping jugular. "Didn't you ever read Tennant Rowe's autobiography?"

"Tennant Rowe?"

More kisses. "Railers—"

"I know who Tennant freaking Rowe is, Jesus."

"Well, he and his husband went at it all over the Olympic Village, and they were on different teams."

"Why would I read that book? I'm a snowboarder," he replied as I lapped at his collarbone.

"Because Rowe is an icon."

"I know, but…" He groaned into another kiss.

"You taste so good, Tian," I coughed out just as the door from reception opened to swat Tian in the back. He huffed in pain. My head snapped up as I readied myself to rip whoever had interrupted us a new asshole. Starry stood there, eyes wide, room key cards in one hand, his carry-on bag over his shoulder.

"Oh, oh shit. Sorry, sorry! Sorry, oh shit, so sorry. I just… you've been gone for twenty minutes. I thought maybe you fell into the pool and drowned. Right. Well, here's your key. See you in the room. Hi." He nodded at Tian, tossed the key to the laundry cart, and then backed out, his face as red as the sleeve on our jackets.

"Fucking A," I mumbled, the fire starting to wane now we'd been busted so horribly. I relaxed my grip on Tian, letting his feet touch the floor. "Be careful. I don't want to be the reason you twist your knee and can't compete."

"You would never be the reason anything bad happens to me," he said, stealing a kiss, his fingertips combing through my beard as he stared into my soul. "We need to talk. There's so much going on here."

"Here in Milan or here in this nook?"

I dragged my hands down his sides, rougher than I meant to, every nerve begging me to grind him into the wall, nails itching to scrape skin, hands too eager, barely held back by a shred of restraint. I'd have to take a cold shower the moment I got to my room. What I'd say to Starry remained to be seen.

"We might be able to sneak some alone time—lock a door, ignore the curfews, get loud, fuck each other stupid until we can't walk straight." Just the thought of it had my cock aching, my blood rushing hot—I was already halfway there just looking at him. "My training schedule, and yours probably, is chaos times ten, but competition hasn't started yet, so maybe tonight we could slip away."

"Yeah, yeah, I'd like that." I also liked the way my fingertips bumped along his ribs. He was so lean yet muscular. My fingers hadn't forgotten the feel of his warm flesh. Touch craved more skin...

"Cool. I'll text you later. I think we can do this." With that perplexing comment, he stole a fast kiss and then wiggled free. "Later."

He slipped away, leaving me hard as a telephone pole and dazed as hell. I removed my TEAM USA jacket, tied it around my waist backwards, and headed to my room to dive into that cold shower, then take a nap, if I could fall asleep. I was pretty wound up, but the dreams of what tonight might bring would be incentive enough to drop my head to a pillow. I'd built a world where there was more of Tian, even romance, but if all there was on offer was sex in dark corners...

Was I ready for that?

Of course I was.

Starry raised an eyebrow when I slunk in. "You wanna talk about…?"

No fucking way.

So, I did what every sane grown man does when faced with his whole world slipping on its axis. I hid in the shower.

TWELVE

Tian

THE BASEMENT GYM IN THE US TEAM COMPLEX WAS massive, the kind of place that could swallow an entire football field, with rooms branching off for every kind of training. In one corner room, the ski team was bent double in a hot yoga class, the windows fogged from their breath. The lighting was all artificial, buzzing overhead in a way that set my teeth on edge. I hated being boxed in under fluorescents when I could have been out on the mountain with snow under my board and fresh air in my lungs, but today was all about flexibility drills, core stretches, bands tugging at my limbs, and rolling out the tight spots so in my first event my body would respond when I asked it to.

Really, I was down here because I was too restless to sit in my room. Team meetings, sponsor schedules, hours with Abel reviewing footage—it was nonstop. All I wanted was ten minutes with Jack. Just enough for me to explain where my head was at, to let him know it wasn't just sex for me, even if that was all he wanted. He might have been satisfied with another night together, but I knew deep down I wanted more.

Brett sprawled on a mat beside me, halfway through a stretch, talking a mile a minute like usual. "Hey, you hear about Roth?" I tried not to think about my biggest rival, because it would just mess with my head, but I was too wound up to stop Brett talking. At least when he was background noise I could stop my brain from working overtime on what had gone down with Jack. On kissing Jack.

On wanting him.

"Mmm," I said as I finished a final rotation on my glutes.

Brett lowered his voice and checked to see if anyone was listening. No one was. Hell, apart from the sweating US skiers, we were the only idiots down here at seven a.m. when there was a perfectly good breakfast waiting upstairs. "Word is he's lining up the same big jump you've been training. Like, exact same rotation, same grab. He wants to throw it in finals." He grinned as though this was gossip and not a direct shot at my Olympic dreams. I felt a surge of adrenaline—half nerves, half challenge—curl hot in my stomach. If Silvan Roth wanted to go head-to-head with me on the same trick, then fine. We'd see who stomped it cleaner when the lights were on and the world was watching.

My turn to take gold.

"I can handle it," I lied, already thinking about how I could push the trick further—add an extra grab, tweak the axis into an off-axis cork, even float a nosebone in the middle spin—anything to make it harder, sharper, something that would set me apart when it mattered.

The door opened and ten men sauntered in, their laughter carrying ahead of them, and I didn't even need to see Jack to know he'd just walked into the room. I felt it—like static in the air, prickling over my skin. Or maybe I'd just wished it hard enough that it became real. My eyes caught Starry first, the massive D-man, lethal in front of the net and cocky as hell. Then I saw Jack, and I knew the exact second he saw me. He was in slim-fitting training gear that clung to him, his steps stuttering just enough to give him away. This time, he didn't look anywhere else, though his glance slid over to Brett, who was staring openly at the new arrivals.

"Is it just me who finds hockey players hot?" Brett whispered, grinning, and I made a show of rolling my eyes at him.

The hockey players split off immediately, some heading to the weight racks for upper-body sets, while others stretched out with resistance bands, their trainers barking instructions. They still had five days before their first game, but no one slacked—they were building strength, keeping sharp, maintaining that balance of power and flexibility. I forced my attention back to my own stretches, to the pull in my hamstrings and the burn in my core, trying to ignore the way my pulse raced every time I risked another glance at Jack.

He tilted his head.

Did he tilt his head?

Am I imagining it?

He spoke briefly with the trainer working with his small group, then pointed toward one of the back rooms. The trainer nodded, clapped him on the shoulder, and moved on. Jack peeled away, sauntering over to one of the side doors without glass, slipping inside and leaving it slightly ajar. From the main floor, it was hidden from his teammates, and Brett was still rambling beside me.

I grabbed Brett's arm. "You didn't see this," I muttered. "Can you watch our backs?"

Brett blinked at me, then nodded, wide-eyed, and I strode off in the same direction, quickening my pace.

I shut the door behind me, heart hammering, but it was Jack who reached past and locked it with a sharp *click*. He turned to me, breath rough, a half-smile nothing like calm tugging at his mouth.

"Yoga," he said quickly, voice low and dark. "Wanna try a pigeon pose with me?" Then he dropped to his knees in front of me before I could answer, shoving me back against the wall.

This wasn't smooth or sweet like in the island. This

was raw desperation and need, his hands hard on me, his eyes burning, and every inch of me answering with the same hunger. His mouth was on me before I could breathe, hot and hungry, and when he dragged my shorts down I buried my fingers in his hair, holding on as he sucked my brains out. The scrape of his teeth, the wet heat of his tongue, it was filthy and perfect, and when he looked up at me with those gorgeous blue eyes, it nearly undid me. My thighs trembled, my head smacked the wall, and still I pushed deeper, needing more, needing him.

I came hard, breathless, shaking as the orgasm tore through me. I slumped, chest heaving, vision blurred, but before I'd even finished dragging air into my lungs, I went to my knees, yanking him close with a rough kiss, tasting myself on his tongue. In a blur, I forced him back until his shoulders hit the mat. I straddled him, kissing down his chest, biting at skin, desperate to mark him, to own this moment. Then I slid lower, between his thighs, and wrapped my lips around his cock, taking him deep, greedy for the taste of him, for the groan rumbling out of his chest as his hands clutched at my hair.

He was rambling, praising, more vocal than I remembered, his words tumbling roughly between gasps —dirty encouragements, choked curses, my name dragged out on his tongue as if he couldn't stop himself. The sound of it made my skin prickle, made me ache to push him further. He stared at me, wide and wild, and every desperate noise he made drove me harder, hungrier, until I wanted nothing but to wreck him completely.

"I've missed... this... want... more..." he panted.

I drove down harder, gripping his hips so tight my knuckles whitened. When he came, he tried to be quiet, but a strangled cry ripped free as he arched up, my throat burning as I gagged while he filled me. He dragged me up for a kiss, messy and urgent, and I collapsed onto him, breathless, laying my full weight across his slick body, loving the way we fit together. To him it might have been nothing but sex, but to me he was my safe place, my hunger and my happiness all at once—and for a single desperate moment I wished he felt it too.

He held me close, and I buried my face in his neck, tasting the salt of his skin, kissing along the line of his throat. His arms wrapped around me so firmly it was as if he'd never let go. But we were done, weren't we? Time to separate, me back to my side of the world, him to his, until next time—if there even was a next time. Only he shuffled to sit up, muscles rippling, taking me with him until I straddled his lap, his back pressed to the wall. Then he cradled my face, eyes fierce, mouth set like he was about to say something that would wreck me.

"We need to talk," he began, voice rough. "No, I need to talk..."

Here it was. The speech. The part where he told me it had been one and done, that he'd fucked his anger out of his system and now he was finished. But then his forehead dropped to mine, his breath hot against my lips.

"I'm listening," I whispered.

He sighed, the sound ragged. "I hate this," he said.

I stiffened. "What? You hate what we're doing here?"

"No—"

"You hated when we were away—"

He cut me off with a bruising kiss. "Stop talking. And no. Fuck, no. I hate that it can't be more. That you don't want it to be more."

I froze. "What?"

His hand pressed flat to my chest, right over my heart. "I feel so much. I missed you so much. This—" His voice cracked. "This isn't just about sex for me."

Before I could answer, there was a knock on the door and Brett's voice whisper-shouted, "Time out, Tian!"

I jolted, scrambling off him. Jack helped me up, then jumped to his feet, masking everything in a second, then he tugged me close, eyes blazing. "I missed you."

I kissed him gently. "I missed you too."

"You did?"

"I did."

"Look, can you get away? To talk. I'll find a place we can go… to talk."

Another knock. "For real, Tian," Brett said, this time louder.

I unlocked the door. "Message me."

He smiled then. "Yeah."

THIRTEEN

Jack

AFTER A BOARD GAME SET IN A HAUNTED HOUSE WHERE I was bisected with a chainsaw by Jimmy Keeney, a forward from Seattle, I wandered the hotel, trying to find somewhere nice to have a meet-up with Tian. Leaving the hotel was doable, obviously, we weren't in lockdown, but we were in training, which meant our coach, Phil Delaney from New York, preferred if we stuck to our routines. Hockey players are creatures of habit so that was fine with me. Also sneaking out to party? Nah. The youngsters could have that bullshit. Give me a good skate, a hearty meal, and a nap before a night game. Since there were no games for us, night or day, for a few more days, I'd happily swap out a game for a cuddle and a chat with Tian.

What was proving hard was finding privacy. I

returned to my room in a sulk and Starry picked it up on the moment I entered.

"You look like you lost your dog," he said, glancing up from his e-reader to me. I liked Starry. He was about my age, maybe a few years younger, but settled. He had a wife, a two-year-old boy, and another on the way. His son had come down with strep the day before they were set to fly over, so his wife and boy were back home.

I dropped to the edge of my bed, a comfortable king on which I slept well. Finding his hazel gaze locked on me, I figured he was okay to talk to. I mean he had walked in on Tian and I going at each other like a couple of rabid vampires.

"Tian," I opened with. He sat up a little straighter and closed his . "We have a history."

"I sort of assumed that," he replied with a slight smile tugging at one side of his mouth.

"Right, yeah, well, I'm bisexual."

"Assumed that as well as you were married to a woman but sucked face with a guy."

I felt my cheeks warming. Talking about my sexuality wasn't something I was comfortable thrashing out with other people. What happened in my bed, and with whom, was not fodder for the media. It was private and between my partner and me. But, sadly, the world loved the hot gossip. And if it involved queer jocks all the better. You'd think things would have improved since Tennant Rowe had shattered the stigma years ago but no, not yet. Pity really that people clung to hatred so fucking tenaciously when they could just be kind.

"Right." I rubbed a thumb over a scarred knuckle. Lots of fights on these old hands. "Well, we're in this weird place. You got a few minutes?"

"I got nothing but time." He placed his e-reader aside to give me his full attention. So, I unloaded on him. Every detail of what had taken place with Tian and me from the first view of him getting on that plane to our time in the laundry nook. He nodded here and there but overall, just sat with his long legs out in front of him and listened. I bet he was a good dad. He had all kinds of patience for ramblings about surfboards, sun lotion, and twinky snowboarders who didn't quite grasp personal space.

When I reached the end, I sighed and then stared at him as if he were a wise man atop a snowy mountain.

"Sounds like you two need to talk," he said, to which I nodded. He slung his legs from his bed, slid his feet into some sneakers, and stood. "Rumor has it there's a horror board game tourney taking place in one of community rooms. I love horror shit. I think I just might go play a few rounds then eat in the hotel restaurant. I'll probably be gone for several hours. Probably at least until quiet hour sets in."

"Starry, I never meant that you had to leave your own damn room. I was just venting."

He patted my cheek. "Let it never be said that Pete

Starinski stood in the path of true love. If you're occupied, come ten p.m., just hang a jock on the doorknob."

"Uhm, no. Thanks, man." I rose to give him a solid bro hug.

He grabbed his jacket and wallet, gave me a wink, and then eased out of the room. I was on my phone texting before the door closed properly. Tian was busy with interviews but could join me in an hour. Which was perfect. I texted him my room number, then put in an order for room service. Since we were both athletes in training, I did my best to keep the dinners healthy. I ordered two plates of spaghetti Bolognese plus extra side salad. Spring water to drink, then for dessert, two of their Greek yogurt berry parfaits. Once that was done, I showered and changed out of my workout gear into something comfortable yet attractive. Then, because I had forty-five minutes to spare and was nervous, I hit up my sister.

"Hey, oh wow, you look nice. Did you trim your beard?" Fiona asked while moving through her apartment.

"Some lady did for pictures back in the States. Are you packing?"

"I am," she said. I'll be in Milan tomorrow afternoon. I'm booked at the Gray Arms which is my favorite place to stay in Milan! Did I ever tell you about the layover that I had once in Milan fifteen years ago with an Italian boxer named Guiseppe?"

"No, and to be honest, I'm not up to hearing about your layovers. Or unders."

She laughed.

"Actually, I need some advice. I ran into Tian here at the Olympic Village and—"

"Tian from the cay whom you refused to talk about after that one night you had too much wine at my place and confessed that you had never felt that way about anyone before? That Tian?"

I had to roll my eyes. "Yeah, that Tian. We sort of had a meetup and things are looking like they might be okay with us. Like…" I rubbed at my hairy cheek. "Like we might be able to work things out but then I think about it and am stumped as to how we could possibly even entertain the idea of maybe being a couple since I'm so much older and—"

"Stop. Stop thinking. Just let it happen."

"I'm scared." Saying that dropped a weight off my back. Hockey players weren't supposed to fear anything but giving my heart to another person who might stomp it into pumpkin pudding? Yeah, that shit was terrifying.

"Oh, honey, I know. Love is terrifying but not everyone is going to treat you as badly as your ex did. Just stop thinking about all the things that can go wrong and focus on what you can make go right."

"Fiona—"

"Now go trim that beard a little more. Oh, and your eyebrows too. Then wine, dine, and sixty-nine him."

"Fiona…"

"I'll be there tomorrow. I expect to see hickeys. Now go. Get moving." She made a shooing motion with her hand then ended the call. Pushy woman. Still, I rushed into the bathroom to tidy up my brows. I was just about done trying to reshape my left brow as I'd gotten a bit wild with the razor when a knock on the door startled me. I nearly whacked half my brow off. There were still twenty minutes until Tian was supposed to arrive. Thinking it was Starry who had forgotten something and didn't have his room key, I opened the door, but there stood Tian. My heart rate tripled just seeing him.

"You're early," I said, opening the door and then stepping to the side to let him in. Starry and I were both pretty tidy, so the suite wasn't a hog pen. I shut it, then stood there just soaking up the scent of his aftershave in the air. He smelled so good. Masculine to the nth. "Dinner will be here soon."

"Cool. Sorry to show up early. They were done with me." He smiled as he peeled his jacket off, then tossed it to a chair by the window.

"I want to kiss you so badly, but I promised myself I would be a gentleman."

Tian's eyes rounded slightly. "Oh—"

"But, I want you to know that I want more than just

sex, so tonight, good food, conversation, and early to bed."

"Not even one kiss?" The pout he hit me with nearly buckled my knees.

"Maybe a goodnight one."

"Stingy," he teased as he took off his shoes and then gestured at the bed. I pointed at mine, and he climbed in.

He opened his arms and I dove onto the bed, then curled around him like a vine, tucking his head to my shoulder as his strong legs tangled with mine. Oh yeah, this was nice. Being naked would be nicer, but this was nice as well. I inhaled the rich scent of his shampoo lingering on his satiny black hair.

"Do you remember our last night on the cay when we lay on the sand and watched the sun go down?" he asked, quietly.

"Of course." I remember wondering how I'd ever give Tian up but knowing I had to, because that was what we'd agreed.

Tian sighed. "I tried to memorize every shade of orange in the sky because I knew we were coming to an end. I've carried that with me for six months. Every night I closed my eyes and saw that sunset, and you smiling down at me."

"You did?"

He rolled over to face me, propping his chin on my chest. "I wish…"

"What?"

"That we hadn't made that stupid deal to just have the time on the cay."

"Agreed," I whispered, and my heart swelled. "You feel so perfect in my arms, Tian."

"I like being here. No..." He paused, and I waited because it seemed as if he wanted to say more. "I *love* being here."

I carded my hand through his hair. "I love being here too."

"How would you feel if we did more of this after we get home?"

I was quiet for a moment, and his eyes brightened with emotion. "Good. Yes. I want that."

He smiled then and shifted a little so he could kiss my chin. "If we do a thing, it will be hard."

"'A thing'?" I dropped a kiss on his hair and sighed out six months' worth of pining. "If we go on a date, that would be dating, right? Unless there's a different term for it now?

"No, we still call it dating, Gramps."

I gave his back a tickle. He snorted and kicked. Our food arrived as we played around. Once I had him pinned, I broke my word and stole a kiss. Just a short one on the tip of his nose, and he hustled off to let the waiter deliver our meals.

We ate in front of the double windows, which were closed to ward off the chilly temperatures. The meal was good, but the company was superlative. Our plates were clean when we returned to my bed with our huge cups of fruit and yogurt.

I sat tight up to his side, dipped my spoon into my parfait, and offered him a bite. Something hot erupted in his gaze as he leaned over, mouth open, to take what I was giving him. A steamy memory of his lips taut around my cock threatened to knock my vow of chivalry aside.

I changed the subject. "You looking forward to the opening ceremony?"

He sighed as his lips pulled the sweet treat from my spoon. My dick was not on board with the chaste shit at all, but I would not be ruled by my penis. Tonight anyway.

"Yeah, it's exciting. You?"

"Yeah, I really am." I fed him another bite. His long lashes had me mesmerized. "I've never been before and probably will never get another opportunity, so I want to drink it all in. I want to live every moment, every second, of my time here to the fullest. And that includes whatever time I can get with you."

"And *after* the games?" he asked, his lips red from the raspberries. I so wanted a taste of those pouty lips, but if I took one kiss, it would lead to others. Many others. All over his body. He yawned and hid it behind his hand. "Sorry, just been a full-on day."

"It's okay." I pulled back what he'd asked me.

"After the games? I hope we can work something out. I still have a couple of months of the season, then playoffs." I was certain we'd make the playoffs, and I wouldn't think any other way. "Will you be free after Italy wraps up, or do you go right out and start competing again?"

He waved off the next spoonful, his head coming to rest on my shoulder. "I'm not sure. Maybe take some time? I'm pretty fucking tired."

I nodded before eating a spoonful of my dessert. His taking time off? Totally understandable. Athletes trained their asses off, competitions and games took their toll, not to mention the pressure of the press and social media. Mental health took a beating just like our bodies did.

"If you took time off, we could maybe spend some time trying to be normal guys who go to dinner or movies or spend time at home, when I'm not playing, which is all the time I know. My ex-wife hated the months of separation." I ran my tongue over a berry seed lodged between my front teeth, sucked it out, and then swallowed it with another bite of dessert. Tian said nothing. Shit. Maybe he was considering not getting involved if he took time off after winning his medal. I had no doubt he would win big. "I know you're not Paula obviously, but—"

The sound of a soft snore flitted up from him. I leaned up just an inch to ease his dessert from his hand.

I placed his glass cup on the nightstand, then wiggled back into place at his side, smiling to myself like a dork as I enjoyed my dessert as well as the weight of Tian sleeping so peacefully at my side. If it were up to me, I'd sit here just like this all night. Talk about besotted…

———

I'D EXPERIENCED A LOT OF INCREDIBLE MOMENTS IN MY life.

Stanley Cup finals, weddings, birthdays, vacations in the Caribbean that changed everything. Walking in the Parade of Nations inside San Siro Stadium was right up there with the top five.

Even though Tian had left my room the night before, I carried with me everything we had said about seeing each other after the Olympics. I'd dreamed about it after he'd left, woken up with good thoughts in my brain, and couldn't shake the happiness all day as we readied for the opening ceremony.

And now I was marching with my team, alongside skiers, figure skaters, and of course, snowboarders. I'd never felt prouder to be American. Tian was in front of me, to the left, so I could watch him smiling and waving. At my right was a speed skater, and at my left was a woman participating in the biathlon. At this moment, we weren't separate sports, we were one team under one flag.

Fireworks lit up the night sky as we circled the stadium to the roars of thousands of fans. My sister was out there somewhere along with Tian's parents. I smiled so widely my cheeks ached when we came to the end of the parade. We then stood through a speech by the president of the IOC and the president of the organizing committee. Flags of various nations waved through the stands as the shouts of thousands floated skyward. The Olympic anthem began to play while a famed Italian opera soprano sang the lyrics. The biathlete beside me started to cry as the Olympic flag was raised. I gave her a small pat on the back and got a weak smile in reply.

Standing facing the Olympic cauldron I felt a surge of excitement and awe raced through me as the flame, which started its trip to Italy in Greece, arrived via one of the world's best alpine skiers who had claimed over twenty medals throughout his illustrious career. We all applauded. The final torchbearer was a secret so everyone here was surprised but seemingly very pleased with Massimo Leone from Rome being the honored athlete.

Many of the American athletes were heading to an off-site celebration at a club called Blue Green 88 where many of the students from Vita-Salute San Raffaele University hung out. The younger guys on the hockey team had coerced Starry and me, officially the elder statesmen of the players, to join them. The club was packed, green and blue lights flashing to the beat of an

Italian dance song. Fiona tugged me into the mix, always a gal who loved to shake her groove thing, and within five minutes I was surrounded by horny young Italian men seeking a dance with my sister. Several I threatened with a fist, four I had to go chest to chest with, and one insisted they would throw themselves over a cliff if Fiona didn't dance with him. I offered to help him with that, but my sister intervened before I could cart the lovesick slob to one of the coastal areas of Italy and boot his ass into the sea. Free of charge.

Thankfully for him, and the other sots circling my baby sister, a certain snowboarder showed up, slinking up to me on the dance floor then taking me by the wrist to a table in the corner.

"You look angry," Tian shouted, dropping down beside me at a small booth with a very sticky table.

"Yeah, horny guys buzzing around my sister," I leaned over to say into his ear. An adorably cute ear I had to admit. "What are you doing out? Don't you have a competition tomorrow?"

He smiled sweetly. I wanted to gather him up and plop him on my lap but that would be pretty scandalous. Instead, I just took his hand and threaded his fingers with mine.

"I do, and I'm heading back to be in bed by midnight."

"Okay, good. You need your rest. Fiona and I have tickets for your events. They're all on my phone."

"Cool. I'll take all the cheering I can get." I gave his fingers a squeeze. My sister arrived then, sweaty and out of breath, without her swarm of admirers. She sat down, tossed her hair over her shoulder, and smiled at Tian.

"So, this must be the man who stole my brother's heart. Fiona." She held out her hand. Tian took it to give it a shake. "It's so nice to meet you, Tian. Jack talks about you all the time. Just so you know it's me who pushed my big brother into the vacation so if you want to offer me homage of any sort I do love fine shoes, designer bags, and small precious gemstones set in platinum."

Tian brought her hand to his lips to kiss her knuckles. Fiona's plucked brows flew to her hairline.

"For having a hand in bringing me and Jack together, there aren't enough shoes, totes, or jewelry in the world to repay you," Tian yelled over the din. Fiona fanned herself with her free hand as if she might swoon. Me? I was way past the swooning stage. Any man who treated my sister like she was a queen had my heart. To be honest, I was pretty sure he had it way before tonight.

The Olympic Village was never truly quiet, not even after curfew. Somewhere a door slammed, laughter echoed, footsteps shuffled past on tired legs. But out here, under the streetlamps throwing golden pools across the paths, it felt as if the world had emptied itself just for us as we walked back to Team USA's base.

Tian's hand brushed mine as we walked, fingers

skimming, testing. I should have pulled away. Cameras, teammates, reputation—any of a hundred reasons to keep space. Instead, I laced our hands together and squeezed.

"You nervous?" I asked softly, my breath clouding in the cold.

Tian huffed a laugh. "About competing tomorrow? Or about getting caught sneaking around with an NHL captain who definitely knows better?"

"Both. But, mostly about you. I don't want to be a distraction."

"You're not." He tugged me toward a bench under one of the lamps. The wooden slats were icy, but I didn't care. I wanted whatever this moment was going to be. "You're... grounding. Like, when everything feels too big, I think about you, and it stops spinning."

He caught me off guard. But I reached out, cupping the back of his neck, pulling him close in the shadows. His forehead rested against mine, heavy with things I wasn't saying.

"Good luck tomorrow," I whispered. "I'll be there, watching, I promise."

The small kiss goodnight wasn't enough, but I'd take what I could get.

FOURTEEN

Tian

Marco Bellini, a former Big Air legend, was the official pundit for too many TV channels to mention, and he was with me and Silvan Roth waiting to be counted in for the introduction to the show and a brief interview. I didn't much like the media attention, but it was the Olympics, and I was here, and I was one of the favorites, so I could give them a little time.

The camera operator counted in, and then a light blinked on.

"Good morning, everyone! Thank you for joining us! I'm Marco Bellini, former Italian Big Air gold medalist, and I'm absolutely fired up to be here for day one of the FIS Snowboard World Cup Big Air event!" he exclaimed, vibrating with energy as the camera zoomed in. "I'm here with the top two seeds for the event, but before I start asking them questions, let's get into it."

He waited as the camera panned to the mountains, and the runs we'd be using, and then back to Marco. "If you're new to this incredible spectacle, let me break it down! Three days of pure adrenaline: qualifiers, semis, and then the grand finale!" Everything he said was layered with so much excitement it was infectious. "Riders can hit speeds of nearly forty miles per hour as they fly down the in-run, launching off the towering kicker, and every one of the death-defying flights they do is called a trick. Every trick has to be both clean and progressive—we're talking mind-bending spins, grabs held as if your life depended on it, and amplitude so big it makes the judges leap out of their chairs." He leaned into the camera as if he were sharing a secret. "Land sloppily and you'll get hammered on points!" Then he waved at us, "But these riders stick it clean, and the scores climb, and with them their shot at Olympic glory!"

He gestured at us. "Here with me today I have Silvan Roth, Team Switzerland, with an Olympic bronze in '18 and a silver in '22, and also Tian-Lei Cai-Wilder of Team USA, fresh off a strong qualifier."

We both said hi, Silvan all cool, me with a small wave and a quick rock-on sign—index and pinkie finger raised—that riders and fans always threw out to show excitement. Marco joined in, but Silvan was too cool to do that and laughed at us both.

Marco turned to Roth. "So, Silvan, looking all serious there!"

"Winning is a serious business," he deadpanned.

"This is your third Olympics. A bronze, a silver, already, so I'm assuming you're going for gold this year?"

Roth grinned. "That's the plan."

"Not if I have anything to do with it." I smirked, earning a chuckle from the small crowd beyond the camera, as well as Marco himself, and a mock glare from Silvan.

Marco beamed at us both. "Gentlemen, before we let you go, let's talk conditions. Viewers at home want to know—what's the snow like today, how's the course running?"

Roth nodded. "Perfect conditions. The powder's packed just right, not too icy, not too soft. It's fast out there, which is exactly how we like it."

Marco turned to me. "And the weather? It looks incredible on camera—clear blue skies, hardly a cloud. How does that affect you when you're up top, ready to drop in?"

"Honestly?" I took the question and grinned. "It's ideal. Visibility is everything. No flat light, no shadows to mess with spotting landings. The mountains look gorgeous, but more importantly, I can see every detail of the course when I'm spinning."

Marco clapped his hands together. "There you have it, folks—perfect snow, perfect weather, and two riders ready to throw down!"

My three jumps had been a mix of safe and ambitious. First, I opened with a switch-backside 1440 melon, clean and controlled, a banker to ensure I was on the board. I even spotted my dad at the bottom of the course, standing just a couple of people away from Jack and his sister. My heart leapt, and I waved at them, grinning so wide my face ached. Dad waved back, his whole face lighting up. The barrier was there for a reason, but before the next heat started, I jogged down, ducked around the rope, and wrapped him in a hug. Security didn't even blink—it was part of the culture here, family meant everything, and riders always got a second to ground themselves. His arms around me, his laugh in my ear, it steadied me more than any pep talk ever could. Then I pulled back, breathless, and I was high on the clean jump and gestured for Jack to step closer. I wasn't going to hug him on camera, but...

"Jack, meet my dad. Dad?" I lowered my voice. "This is *my* Jack."

Jack's eyes widened, and I think he was going to say something, but before I got into trouble, I was ready to climb back up for my next run. This time, I pushed harder with a frontside 1620 mute, big amplitude, but I over-rotated slightly and had to fight for the landing. The adrenaline rush was fierce, the kind that made my vision blur at the edges. For a split second, I felt the board slide out from under me, panic roaring, but muscle memory snapped me back. I wobbled, fought like hell, and somehow pulled it back under control to land safely. My legs shook as I rode it out, heart pounding so hard it drowned out the crowd, relief crashing through me even harder than the jump itself.

I bumped fists with Dad, then Jack and Fiona, no hugs, but fuck, I was high on life. There is nothing like winning a battle with myself.

For the third jump, I came back swinging with a backside 1800 Indy, stomping it clean—the kind of trick that made the judges sit forward. That combination— safety, risk, and redemption—was what landed me in third overall at the end of day one, not a bad place, tucked right behind Silvan Roth in first and a Japanese rider, Renji Sato, in second. I might not be at the top, but I had a solid foundation for what was to come next.

I wouldn't lose my shit on another jump like my second.

Brett was just a ball of sunshine, thrilled with his twelfth-place finish, which was just enough to slide him into the semis. He bounded over to chat with Sato like they were old friends, and even Roth gave him a smile. I watched them, amused, then glanced at Roth.

"Were we that young once?" he asked.

"I'm only twenty-seven," I pointed out.

"And I'm only thirty-one," he said with a shrug, then his smile dimmed. "But still... last Olympics for me, though, right?"

This was his third Olympics, all while I'd been trying so fucking hard to make the big show, attempting to fight my own impulses to try too hard and crashing out. I'd come good for this year, but that sad, wistful note in his voice made me really see the clock ticking for him, and probably me as well. Maybe I could make the team for '30, maybe keep traveling the circuits a few more years—or maybe I retired.

How easy would it be to give it all up? Impossible. Still, the thought crept in. Perhaps I'd coach someday, passing on what I knew. Working with the youngest kids, shaping the next generation. Maybe even settling into a base in the US, closer to my sponsors, closer to the scene... maybe even near Harrisburg, where the Railers team were and where Jack lived. The idea felt both terrifying and strangely comforting.

At the hotel that night, the coaches from each team scattered around the foyer, comparing notes and laughing over coffees. Brett was so high from his result I nearly had to peel him off the ceiling, buzzing around like he'd just won the whole damn event. Not that I was any better—I was just as pumped, the adrenaline from my runs still burning in my veins. We shot the breeze with a few other riders, catching up on news from the other events, the kind of chatter that made the Olympic Village feel alive and connected. And then I caught sight of Jack walking in, shoulders squared, looking every inch the sexy man I wanted. I froze as I saw him heading for the same door we'd disappeared through the first day we got here. He didn't even have to gesture for me to follow; I was already moving. Making some quick excuse to Brett, I strolled in that direction, heart pounding as I trailed after him and got yanked to one side as soon as I reached the laundry nook.

Jack grabbed me, pulling me hard against him, his mouth already on mine before I could breathe. "That was beautiful," he whispered between kisses, his voice kept low, cautious—as if he was terrified that same woman might come storming over to tell us to keep it down again. "Fucking amazing, Tian."

"Thank you."

"You're beautiful."

"Fuck, Jack, seeing you at the end of the jump—"

He kissed me again, harder, his excitement spilling over, and I gave up trying to talk and laughed against his mouth, then swallowed the sound as his tongue slid against mine. What started frantic softened, slowed, became a kiss that lingered, his forehead resting against mine, our breath shared. I pressed into him, our hips grinding, the desperate edge turning into something almost tender. We kissed and rubbed, our eyes locked, and in that moment, it wasn't about medals or points, just about being here, together, wanting each other so badly it hurt.

Jack murmured against my lips, words tumbling out between kisses, praises, and curses that made my skin burn. "So, fucking proud of you... God, you're gorgeous... can't believe what I saw... can't believe I have you here." Every whisper made me shiver harder, made me grind against him with more urgency. My fingers dug into his back as the heat between us spiraled until I couldn't hold back—I lost it first, breaking apart with a muffled cry into his mouth. Jack didn't stop, kissing me through it, until he groaned and followed, clutching me tight as if he'd fall apart without me. Breathless, sweaty, we slumped together, foreheads pressed, our hearts hammering in the same wild rhythm.

I wasn't long back in my room, Brett heading down to the gym, when my phone buzzed with an incoming video call from Dad. I answered, and both he and Mom were peering into the camera in the way that only parents can.

"Amazing day one, son!" Dad boomed, pride dripping from every word.

Mom chimed in, her voice warm and teasing. "Dad said you were incredible out there. We're so proud of you." Then she cut to the chase as all the best moms do. "But more importantly... who is Jack? I mean, we know he's the captain of the Railers and a hockey player—I looked him up—but who is he to you and when do I get to meet him?"

I froze, then grinned so hard it hurt. "He's the man I'm gonna marry," I blurted, then laughed at myself. Because, jeez, we were barely at the start of things, but god, I wanted more.

There was a pause on the line, and then Mom laughed too, delighted. "Oh, sweetheart!"

Dad cleared his throat, but I heard the smile in his voice. "Well, he'd better be worthy of you."

"He is," I said softly, more sure of that in that moment than I'd ever been. "You'll see."

"Dinner, as soon as your event is over, and before his starts," Mom replied.

"Of course."

We said our goodbyes, Mom promising to watch my runs on the highlights that Dad curated so as not to freak her out too much, and then I was on my bed, restless but tired, knowing I needed to get some sleep before tomorrow's day two.

My phone buzzed again just as I was plugging it in to charge. A message this time. Jack.

Jack: Can't make tomorrow's runs. We've got a mandatory media block—press, interviews, all that PR crap they love to shove at us.

Tian: I wouldn't swap you for that.

Jack: Not when you're flying like you did today. Fiona will be there, and I'll be thinking of you, though.

Tian: Good. Maybe I'll throw a trick just for you.

Jack: Just land it clean. Gold looks better on you than bruises would.

Tian: On it.

Jack: BTW, what you said to your dad?

Tian: What?

Jack: About me being your Jack?

Tian: Seemed right at the time

Jack: I like it. Very possessive

Tian: Asshole

Jack: Now get some sleep, Tian. Second day tomorrow.

Tian: xx

Jack: XX

I set the phone down, smiling so hard my cheeks hurt, my body still buzzing with adrenaline and heat.

Day two of the Big Air was all about tightening the field. Another three runs, each rider trying to outdo themselves and secure a spot in the finals. The conditions held perfect—clear skies, packed snow—and the crowd was louder than ever. I landed two of my three clean, upping my average and pushing myself into second place overall by the end of the day. Not bad company to be in, right behind Silvan Roth with Renji Sato breathing down my neck. Brett didn't make it out of day two, but he didn't seem that worried, just excited. Oh, to be that young.

And then it was day three—the final showdown.

Each of us had three runs, but this time only the top two scores counted, so consistency mattered as much as risk. I was ready for it, my body humming with nerves and adrenaline, knowing this was where Olympic dreams could be secured or shattered.

The last jump was all or nothing. I dropped into the in-run faster than I ever had, board humming across the packed snow, and when I hit the kicker, I threw every ounce of myself into it. A backside 1980 indy, five and a half full rotations, and in the middle of it I added the twist I'd been saving—switching the grab from indy to tail mid-spin, a split-second adjustment that made the whole thing twice as technical. The world blurred, the roar of the crowd vanished, and it was just me spotting the landing, knees tight, body screaming from the G-force. I hit the snow solid, legs like shock absorbers, arms up clean. The crowd erupted, and my breath came ragged as I rode it out to the corral.

Jack was there today, next to my dad, both whooping and hollering.

Sato and I were vying for silver, with Sato already having completed his final run—Silvan had already sewn up an untouchable gold.

As soon as the scores flashed on the board, I knew.

Silver was mine.

FIFTEEN

Jack

THE NEXT DAY WAS PACKED WITH HOCKEY PRACTICE.

While I loved the sport to death I also longed to be with Tian. Yes, I was greedy. I knew he was doing the press circuit with his shiny silver medal and his parents. And I was super happy for him to be getting the accolades that he deserved. Still, I wanted him at my side whenever I wasn't on the ice. So yeah, greedy Jack being greedy.

It helped that we'd put in an intense hour on the ice early in the morning to work on getting our lines to gel. I knew most of the guys here but knowing them and playing with them were two different things. Starry and I were paired up which was cool. We'd bonded over our time here listening to each other fart in our sleep. Plus, he was easy to get along with and knew about Tian and me, which made it comfortable. I could share the excitement of his medal while bragging how proud I was of him without getting funny looks.

Coach Delaney was a defensive-minded coach, so he was working to construct a team from the net out with a strong emphasis on structure, discipline, and seeking a strong defensive mindset from all five men on the ice. Lots of drills around neutral zone traps, shot blocking, position over possession, and frustrating our opponents. This was where Starry and I excelled if I dared to toot my own horn. We could suffocate the other team's offense, which forced them to take low-quality shots far from the net. Coach Delaney, a retired D-man, worked us hard and expected results.

"Remember, our number-one challenge is going to be Canada. Yes, the Swiss, Finns, and Swedes are strong, but they don't have the firepower that Canada has. I'm not a pretty man," he told us at the end of our first team skate, making us chuckle. He was right. He wasn't a pretty man. Too many fights and broken noses to be called pretty, kind of like me and Starry. "I don't need a pretty win. I'm happy to win ugly. Keep those Canucks from our zone, grind their pretty boy speedsters down, and always be disciplined. Now, go shower. You all stink. And meet me and Coach Parkes back here at three to show our support for the women's team as they take on Germany in their quarterfinal."

We filed into the locker room, chatting, and I dived on my phone the moment I could wade through the throngs of sweaty men eager to talk hockey. I ended up having to go sit in a stall in the men's room for five minutes of privacy.

Jack: Hey, it's your Jack.

Tian: Hey my Jack. How was your skate?

Jack: Good. Lines are looking sleek; coach is pushing us hard.

Tian: Excellent. We're having lunch in about thirty minutes at a chic little place Mom found online. Want to join us?

Jack: Yeah, I'd love that. Can we bolt after that to go cheer on the USA women's hockey team?

Tian: Hell yeah!

Jack: Perfect. See you in a bit. Send me directions.

I raced through the shower, jogging out of the arena with wet hair. Not a great idea as it was chilly as hell, but a cold scalp would be worth it. Tian and I were grabbing every minute we could from here on out. Hockey was about to kick into high gear with games every other day. Sometimes there were four games jammed into one day, which was insane, but we had only so much time, so it was balls-to-the-wall.

Using a popular app to get a ride, I was at the little restaurant on a cramped side street in downtown Milan in no time. Tian and his parents were sipping something cold when I arrived. His mother was delightful, his father funny, and Tian was… well, Tian was everything. The meal was outstanding. Fettuccine with shrimp, and cannoli for dessert. I was stuffed. Tian patted my belly a time or two, but I wasn't too worried about eating something rich while training so hard. I'd work it off.

With a peck on his mother's cheek and a firm handshake with his dad, we had to leave them to watch the USA women's team quarterfinal game. It wasn't mandatory to attend the games or events of other teams from your country, but it was a common practice. Since Tian and I were Team USA, we got in without paying. There was a seating area set aside, first-come, first-served, which was why Coach wanted us here early. Tian and I got some looks, nothing too gawky, as we weren't holding hands or anything like that. Not that I didn't want to, but we hadn't even discussed our relationship, let alone what, when, or if we would announce we were dating.

Starry waved us over, so we sat beside him. I gave Tian a fast intro to our team and our head coach before settling back to watch an amazing game where our women's team won big and moved onto the semifinal round in three days against France.

After the game, we spent some time in the Olympic Village, had dinner with a few other hockey players, and then had to go our separate ways. I managed to steal a kiss from Tian, in a damn men's room, before heading to my room. Sneaking a kiss sucked, big time, but until we had our lives figured out, we were playing things super low-key. Not getting laid was supposed to be good for an athlete, they used to say. Pent-up aggression and all that silliness. No one really believed that nonsense anymore, but I wouldn't mind a tiny bit of extra belligerence heading into our opening round.

In a way I felt sort of bad for Latvia.

I wasn't sure if it was the old BS about backed-up semen making you more combative or if it was the rush of being in that navy blue with red- and white-accented sweater, but I was taking no fucking prisoners. Coach D wanted defense; he was getting defense. Starry and I were knocking men off their skates like they were bowling pins, and we were the red, white, and blue balls. Since I did have blue balls, it all fit.

We were up three-nothing in the first period. The shift to NHL-sized rinks worked fine for us as we were used to the smaller size. The European teams were still trying to adjust to not being able to execute the fancy passing plays that wider ice allowed them to run. Also, and this was fun, the smaller rink favored physical play. Latvia seemed to be having trouble with the North

American intensity of hits, so we were causing more turnovers, which frustrated them and led to more penalties.

Case in point was taking place now. Andris Ozios was about to lose his shit. I could see it in his eyes as he tried to throw a hip check into Starry, which missed by a mile. I chuckled as I skated past, tossing out a chirp as I whizzed past him, picking himself up.

"And I thought missing the broad side of a barn was just an old saying," I said around my mouthguard. I'd not been sure if Ozios would even understand me, but when his stick found its way into my skate and I hit the ice hard, I had to assume that the forward for Latvia spoke English.

I got to my skates, smiled at the Latvian arguing with the ref, and made my way to the bench for a sip of cold water and a round of ass pats from my teammates. Short tempers made for stupid mistakes. We could hear the Latvian coach shouting at someone, not sure who, as I didn't speak Latvian, but probably me, the ref, or maybe the gods. Whatever, I slammed down some water, gave my head coach a wink, and skated back out for my forty-five seconds of fun.

We had some firecracker forwards on our team, the best of the best, and within ten seconds we were in the Latvian offensive zone swarming their beleaguered goalie. After a blistering shot from a young forward I only knew as Peppy from Dallas, the puck bounced off the goalie's chest as I used my weight to gently maneuver a Latvian defenseman out of the way. Things then went a little tits up, as the Brits say. I spied the puck lying in front of the Latvian's goalie's legs in the blue ice. With a player on my back, literally, I flopped to the ice to try to poke the puck through that gaping five hole.

The guy on my back was not having it. The goalie was not having it. I, on the other hand, was having all of it. I swiped at the puck as another body crashed down on me and watched from my vantage point of cheek pressed to cold ice as the puck skittered through thick pads to just inch over the line. Goal horns blew, fans roared, the guy on my back drove his elbow into my right kidney. Then he hit me with a fist. Right in that same poor kidney. It hurt big time. Like hurt so big I nearly blew my cookies. Whistles blew and whoever it was got the boot from the game, according to the refs yelling at whoever to leave the ice. There's no fighting in the Olympics, not that cheap shots to a man's renal organs was a fair fight.

I got to my skates, sore as hell, but gladly took the back poundings from my teammates for that goal. My flank was on fire, but I was not going to let a little jab take me out of this event. They'd have to scrape me up from the ice in those bright snow shovels the ice teams use to get my old, battered ass off this ice. I did take a small sit, just until my next shift, to drink some water.

"Now *that* was ugly hockey!" Coach yelled as he thumped my shoulder sending hot flashes of pain down my side to my rib and hip where the bruise was probably already forming. "Well done, O'Leary. I want to see more of that dedication and grit, men!"

I smiled and nodded, wiped my nose on my sleeve, and took one more gulp of water before throwing myself back out there. Hockey games weren't won by quitters. As Herb Brooks once said, "Risk something or forever sit with your dreams." I'd risk my body for this team and that gold medal. My heart was already on the line, so I guess I was risking it all for my dreams.

THE NEXT MORNING MY DREAMS WERE MOSTLY ABOUT A heating pad, ibuprofen, and checking for blood every time I hauled my sore ass out of bed to piss. So far so good on the piss. Otherwise, I felt like someone had hit me in the kidney with a two-by-four.

"You really should call the team doctor," Starry said for the tenth time since we'd woken up after our trouncing of Team Latvia.

"It's good. I'm fine. I've had worse pain stubbing my toe," I lied like a big sore rug. "Just give me a few minutes to get with the program."

"Rock head," he mumbled as I moaned and groaned my way to a sitting position.

"Hey, winners don't win if they quit," I ground out while trying to ease my arm into a T-shirt without another whimper.

"Obviously. Will you at least skip morning skate to rest? We don't play again until tomorrow, so you're totally cool to take a down day."

Jesus the man was stubborn.

"Nope, if I skip morning skate Coach will rip me a new asshole. A hot shower, some food, and a few Advil and I'll be right as rain."

What Pete said as he entered the bathroom with his cell I didn't fully catch. Part of it sounded like hardheaded pecker but I could be mistaken. I'd just made it to the little couch by the window when someone knocked on our door. I could hear the shower running and Starry's questionable musical selections blaring, so I old man-walked to the door to peek out the peep hole. There stood Tian, rumpled and sleepy, hair all at cross ends.

"Hey," I said after unlocking and opening the door. "You're up early."

"I got a call from your roommate." He eased in as I did my best impression of a carp lying on the bank. "You're in pain."

"Starry called you? How did he get your number?" I asked as I began plotting how to sneak into the bathroom so I could flush the toilet while he showered. That would show him. "I'm fine just a little—Hey! Stop that! Personal boundaries!"

He tugged the back of my shirt up. I was too sore to lift my arm properly to swat him away. His hiss made me cringe inside.

"Fuck, Jack, that looks awful."

"It's just a bruise. I'm going to kick Starry in the balls."

"You can't lift your leg that high. Come sit down." He eased an arm around me as if I were some old man who might fall over. I leaned into him just so he felt good about being a nosy and overprotective lover. "You should *not* play for a few days. What did the team doctor say when he saw this last night?"

"Take some aspirin, apply heat, let me know if you piss blood or puke." I'd not told the team physician I was in pain so that was all a lie but a good lie because it was based on truth. I'd had bruised kidneys before. I'd had bruised everything before. You didn't play hockey for a living and not end up with injuries. If you did you weren't playing hard enough, or so one of my college coaches had preached.

"Hmm," Tian said as we made our way to my bed. I sat back down with a grunt. "Can I get you to at least let the doctor look at it?" He sat down beside me, his hand on my thigh. "Please?"

"Tian, baby, I'm really touched that you're worried, but it's nothing. Honestly, I'm just stiff and sore but that will go away with a nice heat wrap and massage after skate."

"I think the doctor should look at it," he replied.

"Well, I think it's fine, and it's my body, so what I say goes."

"Do I need to call Fiona?"

I gasped. It hurt. I stared at him in shock. "Don't you dare."

"Then let the doctor look at it."

"Are you always this fucking bossy?"

"Yes, when I care about someone. Now call the doctor, or I'll call Fiona."

"How does everyone I know have each other's phone numbers? What the fuck did I fucking miss, and hand me my fucking phone so I can call the fucking team doctor."

"That was a lot of fucks," Tian said as he reached up to pluck my phone from the nightstand. "We kind of reached out to each other here and there. Making new friends. That's what the Olympics are about."

"Uh-huh," I muttered as I fumbled through the pages of files, numbers, and contact info on my phone until I found the one for the team doctor and dialed it. "Also, I say fuck a lot. I'm a hockey player. Oh, hey, Doc, Jack O'Leary. I have a small, little, tiny bruise on my back near my kidney that's a whisker on the sore side. Should I take some aspirin and use a heating pad, or should I lie down on the floor and just expire? What? No, I was being a smart ass. It's nothing too bad. No, no blood in my urine. Yep, lots of fluids, bed rest. We have a morning skate today, and Coach… okay, well, sure if you think I should take the day to rest. I know we play Denmark tomorrow. It'll be fine by… Sure, I can let you look at it tomorrow morning at practice. Yep, sure, no, yes, okay. Yep, thanks, Doc."

I ended the call and then flipped my phone to the nightstand. "Well, what did he say?" Tian prompted just as Starry broke out into an off-tune rendition of "Love on the Rocks" that made my sore back even sorer.

"Rest today, let him evaluate it in the morning. So, what the hell am I supposed to do all day stuck in this stupid hotel room?" I grumbled, put out with everyone and everything. If I missed tomorrow's game, I was going to be—

"I can hang out with you. Here. Alone. In this bed…" The tone of his voice and the tiny touch of his finger to my thigh drove all my mutterings out of my head. "I mean if you want to be stuck here with me all day."

I threw my hands into the air. I knew when I was beat. "I'm happy as a fucking clam at high tide to spend the day with you." That was the truth. One whole day with Tian locked in a hotel room? Uhm, yes, please and thank you. "I'm still mad at the three of you." I knew I had no reason to be mad at my sister, but once she found out, she would nag, and then I'd have reason, so I was pissed preemptively.

"That's okay, be mad." He patted my face, stole a kiss, and then told me to lie down so he could pamper me for the day.

Turns out Tian wasn't only a fabulous athlete, but he was also one hell of a nurse. The sponge bath he gave me was *exceptionally* memorable.

SIXTEEN

Tian

WE'D KEPT EVERYTHING SOFT AND LOW, A JOKEY BED bath had been less washing, and more me caging Jack and blowing him with all the care and sweetness I could muster, the kind of closeness I craved when everything outside these walls was noise and pressure. Jack had come undone in my mouth, his hand tangled in my hair, the sound of his release a muffled groan I wanted to hold onto forever. But even that tenderness had been too much. When I slid up beside him and kissed the sweat on his cheek, he winced, the pain obvious. That was when I knew something wasn't right.

"Shit, I'm sorry," I whispered, regret clawing at me. "I shouldn't have pushed you."

"I'm fine." He leaned in, brushed his mouth over mine with a shaky kiss. "Give me a second and I'll return the favor," he joked, but when his eyes slipped shut, the color drained from his face. He looked so damn pale it scared me.

"Jack?"

"Five seconds, that's all I need."

"I don't need anything."

He smirked faintly, stubborn even through the pain. "I'm blowing you whether you want it or not. I want my mouth on you, I want to kiss you, I want all of you." His eyes rolled a little, and he placed a hand to his forehead. "Wow, head rush," he said.

"You're not well. Talk to me, Jack."

"I'm fine." His voice cracked into something softer, then he tried to lighten it with a crooked grin. "Hell, I'll even sing the national anthem if that'll convince you I'm fine."

I knew the second he tried to laugh it off that it was bad. He tried to roll to sit up and went white as paper as the movement tore a gasp from him. My stomach knotted with fear when I saw the bruise had spread, ugly purple and black, blooming from his ribs down over his flank and creeping toward his hip, the kind of mottled bruise that looked like spilled ink spreading under his skin. I'd seen bruises, hell, I'd had bruises as bad as this on my limbs, but never this bad on my torso.

"Fuck, Jack, that looks bad."

He smirked faintly, trying to play it off. "I've had

worse; it's nothing," he lied, moving slowly until his feet were on the floor, tugging the sheet up as if he wanted to hide the bruise.

"That's not nothing, Jack. That's your body telling you it's serious," I shot back, unable to keep the fear out of my voice.

He waved a hand as if brushing away my words, but even that small gesture made him grimace. "I've played with worse," he added, as if he wanted to stop me following this train of concern to the inevitable conclusion. "I'm playing," he added.

I understood playing through pain. I understood the focus, the absolute instinct to push past the hurt for the sake of the game, for pride, for the team. But this wasn't the kind of pain you fought through. This wasn't right, and every instinct in me screamed that if he kept ignoring it, it could cost him more than hockey.

I scrambled off the bed to help him up, and he leaned way too much on me, rigid with pain, and he didn't let go, all the way to the bathroom.

"It's okay, you can go," he muttered, clearly embarrassed. I crossed my arms over my chest and stayed put.

"You want me to just walk away while you bleed inside?" I shot back.

"Christ, Tian, do you have to watch me piss too?" he snapped, and the edge in his tone stung.

"If that's what it takes to make sure you don't collapse in here, yeah, I'll damn well watch," I retorted.

He shot me a look, sharp and cutting. "Fucking you doesn't mean you get a say in what I do on the ice."

The words hit like a slap, and I inhaled, stung but refusing to back down. "Maybe not. But caring about you does. And I'm not going to shut up and watch you wreck yourself just to prove how tough you are."

His jaw tightened, fury flashing in his eyes, then dimming to exhaustion. "Fuck, Tian. I didn't mean that," he whispered at last, eyes closing, sagging back against the wall, pale and sweating.

"I know you didn't."

"Just give me five minutes to—"

"No, Jack. I'll back you playing again, I'm in your corner—but you have a life to live, Jack. If you endanger yourself, we don't just lose the game. We lose you." I paused. "*I* lose you."

That broke through his stubbornness, his shoulders sagging in reluctant surrender. He managed to force a weak stream, and the moment the pink swirled into the basin, he slumped forward into my hold. "Fuck," he said hoarsely, trembling against me.

My stomach dropped. "Jack," I said, planting myself in the doorway, "I'm calling the doctor. Now."

He swore, muttering about stubborn boyfriends and overprotective snowboarders. "It's fine. Just a little color—"

"Blood is *not* a thing you play through." My voice came out sharper than I intended, but I didn't care what he thought. I guided him back to the bed and picked up the phone, scrolling to the team doctor and explaining. Within five minutes, the doctor was in the room, and his expression tightened the second he saw the bruise. A quick exam, some pointed questions, and then the verdict landed like a hammer.

"Renal contusion," he said. "Renal contusion, aka kidneys bruised to hell. You're not playing for at least the next four games. Bed rest, fluids, ibuprofen, and heat for the pain. Monitor urine, daily reassessment. No exceptions."

"How long, Doc?" Jack asked.

"Seven to ten."

"Fuck," Jack swore, then started to argue, but the doctor cut him off with a look.

"Push this and you risk permanent damage. You'll be lucky if you're cleared for the final."

That silenced Jack. For once.

I threaded my fingers through his, squeezing hard. "Then we'll do everything right," I said. "Because you're making that final."

The door opened, Starry came in, standing at the door, and stared in shock. His eyes darted from Jack, slumped against me, to the strained way I was holding him. "Jack? What's wrong?" he asked, his voice low, already knowing it wasn't good.

"Out four games," I said.

"Nothing serious," Jack said at the same time.

"Which is it?" Starry asked, moving to one side to let Doc out.

Jack hung his head. "Three to four games."

"But he'll be at the final," I added quickly, meeting Starry's gaze.

Jack shot me a grateful look, and I squeezed his hand.

"He will be," I promised, more to Jack than anyone else.

THE NEXT GAME WE HAD TO WATCH FROM THE ROOM. Starry had switched rooms to give us our space, and I hadn't moved from Jack's side. We watched movies, I read, Jack slept, and all the time I was right there, helping him with whatever he needed. The only time I had to leave was for a sponsor meet, and I hurried back so fast I nearly fell up the second flight of stairs. Fiona visited once, bringing light and laughter into the quiet gloom, but even she couldn't make it easy.

Playing Denmark should have been routine, but the worst part of it was how Jack tried to engage at first, forcing comments and the occasional joke, then slowly ran out of steam. He grew quiet, eyes fixed on the screen, disappointment written in every line of his face. I stayed pressed close, willing him not to notice me watching him fade. Thank fuck the USA were five to two up by the end of the second period. All they had to do was keep it tight, shut it down, and the win would be theirs. Jack's lips curved in a faint smile when the horn sounded, but I could see how much it cost him to even hold that.

We put on *Miracle*, a film we'd both seen a million times, but it had become our snuggle movie, the one with heart that always pulled us close. I'd rearranged the second bed in the room weeks ago into more of a sofa, cushions and pillows piled high, so we curled into it together. I even asked Fiona to smuggle us popcorn, and when she dropped it off with a wink, Jack grinned like a kid.

"I can quote this whole scene," he said as Herb Brooks barked at his team.

"Same," I shot back, tossing popcorn at him.

He caught a piece, laughed, and leaned in to kiss me, the taste of salt and butter on his lips. "Thank you," he whispered. Herb's voice seemed to merge into nothing as he cradled my face, and I straddled his lap. "You're doing this with me, and stopping me from going mad…"

"I wouldn't be anywhere else." I loved him, although I hadn't said it yet. I didn't know what I was waiting for, but the timing didn't seem right. He was injured, exhausted, leaning on me for everything, vulnerable, and sad. No, it wasn't the right time to tell him. Not yet. And he hadn't said it to me either, but one day I knew I'd tell him, and then he could let me know how he felt.

Just not yet.

We kissed a little, but that was all Jack was up for, and I was good with that as we slid back to snuggling.

"You know what the best part of this movie is?" he asked.

"What?"

"Snuggling up to you while we watch it."

We spent the night that way—watching, quoting lines, stealing kisses, and sharing mouthfuls of popcorn until the bowl was empty and we were drowsy in each other's arms.

Best night, along with all the other best nights. From sunsets on a cay to snuggling in a hotel room, we'd had so many.

I love you, Jack O'Leary. I love you.

By the time we played Sweden, Jack had improved a lot. Still in pain, still bruised, but at least he was staying awake, and he'd moved onto the miserably irritable stage. This time, we'd managed to get down into the locker room, though that came with obstacles—so many people wanted to talk to him. He tried to engage, throwing out comments on the defensive coverage, barking a quiet suggestion to one of the youngest guys skating by, and every single one of them listened. He wasn't the captain of Team USA, nor an alternate, but he knew what he was talking about, and respect carried in every nod that came back his way. Still, the effort drained him, and after the second period, we retreated to the room. We ended up scraping a 3–2 win and were through to the quarterfinals, Germany in our sights.

Jack was brighter for the Germany game, staying all three periods and keeping up a steady commentary, leaning into me every so often when the pain caught up. He joked about lazy backchecking, teased the goalie's rebound control, and muttered strategies under his breath as if he couldn't help himself. I loved every second of hearing his hockey brain at work, even as I kept an arm ready to steady him. The USA pulled out a hard-fought win, and when the horn sounded, Jack's eyes were bright despite the bruises. Canada cruised past Czechia in their own quarterfinal, and the way things were shaping up, it was clear—we could be heading toward a USA–Canada final. Just the semis to survive first.

Sweden was the game from hell. Jack was almost healed, itching to get back on the ice, even doing some light skating in the mornings. The doc had said seven to ten days, and Jack had counted every hour—seven was enough in his mind. He was desperate to make that final game. But sitting through Sweden had him furious at himself. The defense wasn't gelling, we were 2–1 down at the end of the second, and he was pacing like a caged animal.

"I should be out there," he muttered, fists clenching. "They're leaving gaps a mile wide."

"Doc said no," I reminded him.

"Doc doesn't see what I see. One more shift and I'd shut that down." His voice cracked with anger, his jaw tight.

"You'll shut Canada down in the final," I said. "Right now, you heal."

He swore under his breath, eyes burning into the ice as if the numbers on the scoreboard might change if he stared hard enough. "I'm useless sitting here."

"You're not useless," I countered. "They listen to you. Every word."

He fell quiet, still furious, but his hand crept into mine, and he didn't pull away even as Team USA fought hard and long and pulled out a win in the last minute, a desperate rush saw one of our forwards pull off a slick toe-drag around the defense and roof the puck top shelf. The whole bench erupted, the crowd went insane, and even Jack forgot to be angry for a heartbeat, his grin wide as he shouted with the rest of us.

Fuck, Jack, I love you.

When the doc cleared him to play in the final against Canada, Jack smiled and nodded, pleased and excited, and I fought down the fear of him getting on the ice and someone from the Canadian team pummeling him, knowing he'd been hurt. The injury had been kept under wraps, but shit, the video of it happening was out there.

Taped up, he was ready. I had a rink-side view, and when he warmed up, he skated toward me, grinned, and I'd never seen him so happy.

He pressed his gloved hand to his heart, then to his lips, and I knew right then.

Surely, Jack loves me back.

SEVENTEEN

Jack

_____

SOMETIMES THE SMALLEST THINGS MAKE THE BIGGEST impressions.

Listening to the national anthems of the US and Canada being played as I stood with my teammates was surreal. A memory I would cherish forever if we won gold or came away with silver. Just being here, suited up, after having to sit on the sidelines was monumental.

So, while this was a memorable moment to carry with me always it was the short little moment at the glass with Tian that was burrowing into my heart where it began to take root. Now was not the time to be romantically daydreaming but when he had looked at me I saw so many things in his gaze. Pride, yes, obviously, but something more. A depth of emotion telling me he loved me, with a ferocity that matched my own feelings for him.

Knowing I should be focused on my game I pushed the emo stuff aside. This was hockey. Big things were about to play out. USA vs Canada for the gold. It had been quite a few years since our boys had brought home the gold. There had been some lean years for our teams, both men's and women's, so we were hungry. We had to bring the gold home. The women's team had done it, so it was up to us to make it a double medal gold bonanza. I hoped my kidney was ready for what might come. I'd been cleared to play by several doctors then wrapped up like a saloon girl. My waist was so cinched I could appear on *Drag Race*. No hog body for old Jack. I'd taken all the precautions and felt good. Sure, there were some twinges when I moved a certain way but not enough to keep my ass on the bench. Singing along to our anthem, I felt as if this was perhaps a prelude to something monumental. Like a change was on the horizon. Not that I'd not experienced lots of change over the past few years. Now, though, there was a brightness to the future that I'd not felt in… well, I couldn't recall when. What the change was I couldn't say but it had to include Tian. Somehow, someway. I was not about to go back to the no-contact days. Nope. That was not an option. We'd work something out…

"Hey, O'Leary, they're singing "O, Canada" now," Starry whispered in my ear.

"I know. I'm singing it to show a sportsmanlike

respect with the Canadian team," I lied like a rug. Starry rolled his eyes.

"Okay, men, this is our game. The Canadians are all flash. They're nowhere near ready to take us on! I need you all to go out there and show them what we can do!" Coach yelled as he stalked up and down the bench, his tie already askew. By the end of the game, it would be a tangled mess from him using it to express himself. Tie talking. Coach spoke it well. "I want everyone tight to their man. Limit their inside passes. I want every one of you to keep their captain tangled up. He's one of their best forwards and they know we know it. Protect the net and fight like junkyard dogs in the corners."

We hit the ice like a pack of mongrels facing off against a pack of purebreds. Yeah, the Canadians had won gold in this sport way more often than we had. The Soviet Union had more gold than the US. A long time had passed since that famous game in Lake Placid.

I drifted slowly to the left, settling in behind the blue line near a winger. Starry positioned himself behind the center, hoping we'd win the faceoff. Then we could react defensively or offensively depending on who won. The men in red sweaters won, their captain snapping the puck to one of his wingers. Off they went. The fuckers were fast—lightning fast, with skating moves that would challenge all our defensemen throughout all three periods.

I caught up with the man with the puck, and using

my shoulder, introduced him to the boards to the right of our goal. He grunted. I kicked the puck free then shuttled it out of our zone to our resident speedster, Tony Pritchard, aka Pritch, the second-highest scorer in the league coming into the Olympic break. Pritch tore down the ice to take a shot on goal the Canadian goalie had to work hard to block.

That breakaway was special. Not because it was a thing of fucking beauty but because it seemed to set a trend, a precedent, blaze a path, create a benchmark. Call it what you wished but something seemed to overtake our team. We didn't play perfect hockey. The Canadians were too slick and strong to not be robbed of the puck or sneaking in quality shots. Even with my back voicing its opinion about this much use even that still ugly contusion had to admit we were beyond in sync. We were playing all-out, balls-to-the-wall, ugly hockey.

Going into the first intermission we'd held the Canadians to five shots on goal. I felt it. The hits I gave as well as the ones I received. No one was seemingly targeting my kidney area but a few of the checks rattled not only my teeth but my poor kidney. One, delivered by a powerhouse of a French-Canadian defenseman near the end of the period, shook me right down to my toenails. Clean check. A thing of beauty. I planned to return the favor at the first opportunity.

When we hit the ice to start the second, things were

still sitting at a goose egg each. This period was always a bit of a bitch. The long change was felt by all. Skating that longer distance added to fatigue, which led to fuckups. I nearly lost my man midway through and had to take a penalty to stop him from breaking away. Coach was not impressed. I wasn't either to be honest but if you gotta trip a dude to save a high quality scoring chance then you trip a dude. The Canadian captain knew he had drawn me into that trip, but he wasn't a showy type. He didn't have to be. He led his team into a power play that cost us a goal.

Coach read me the riot act when I made the skate of shame back to our bench. An ass reaming I deserved. My body was not up to par, not wholly. My back ached like a rotten tooth, but I was playing on despite the aches. A bruise did not keep a hockey player on the bench. I'd seen other guys skate with punctured lungs, broken bones, and busted noses. I'd been known to yank a loose tooth from my mouth, rinse and spit, and go back out for my next shift.

Now, though, I had something to prove. Even if I was old and battered like a farm horse I could still plow a field. Starry and I amped things up. We played old-style defense, skating right on that edge where the refs would give us looks but couldn't call us on anything as we were keeping our skates and sticks on the ice. Like the good noodles that we were. No check went unfinished. No man left uncovered. We fucking blanketed the Canadian offense for ten minutes, our alternate captain pulling a slashing call with three minutes left from a weary Canada player. That led to a goal for our team that carried us into the third tied one to one.

I gulped energy drinks, downed four Ibuprofen, and sat with a heating pad tucked into the back of my hockey pants as Coach gave us our orders. Simple orders. Keep playing ugly. I gave Starry a wink that he returned. Ugly we could do.

With seven minutes in the third it was ugly that did the deed. Thankfully I was on the ice with Starry and our top line, buzzing around the Canadian net like irritated hornets when Dave Killings, a winger from Seattle, took a sloppy shot on goal. Marleau, the Canadian goalie, batted it away with his glove back out into play. Pritch found the puck as it landed, drew back and let the black rubber fly. It hit a Canadian player in the shin which changed its trajectory toward the net. The goalie flailed at the puck as it soared over his left shoulder but couldn't make the save. The red lamp lit. The USA backers—Tian, his folks, and my sister among the hundreds wearing our colors—roared. We fell on Pritch along the boards, slapping his back, patting his helmet, and whooping like demented hyenas. Getting people to the front of the net was never a bad thing. It wasn't a slick, beautiful goal. It would not win any sports writer awards or accolades. It was butt-ugly, but it was a goal. And that, at the end of the day, was all that mattered.

I'd never known seven minutes to take so damned long. The Canadians did not back down. They came out with a fire under their asses that ran us ragged. They were firing from every angle.

"Fuckers are shooting from the fucking concession stands," I grumbled, limping off the ice after blocking a shot with my knee. That was going to need ice. My whole body was going to be nothing but a contusion. Pretty romantic to gaze at when Tian and I were ferreted away by my sister to some secret getaway in Milan. Had no clue where we would spend our two days, but Fiona was certain it would please. She'd brought us together so I was sure she would do us good for this little break from the world. Lord knows we both needed a recharge.

I tossed my helmet to the floor to wipe my head with a towel. The trainer asked if I was all right. I said I was then I shoved my helmet back on to be ready for the next line change. My sight darted between the on-ice action and the clock above center ice. The final two minutes were sheer chaos, but we held tight. We guarded our net as if it were our sister's chastity. When the final five seconds ran out, things got more than a little madcap. They veered right into insanity.

The buzzer sounded and for a moment I heard silence and then...

We'd done it!

Gold!

We rolled out onto the ice, burying our goalie, who'd stood on his head to not allow one of those blistering shots in, to celebrate. We met on the ice to shake hands with the Canadians, who were obviously disappointed but polite as always.

It was a blur of activity and celebration that ran right into the medal ceremony. The Canadians went first. We went second, our names called out as had been the case for the silver medalists, as a representative of the Olympic committee draped a gold medal over our sweaty heads, then shook my hand. The American anthem was played once more, then we gathered at center ice, a large flag with us, to have our pictures taken.

Ramped up on the victory, pride flowing through me, I was sure I wouldn't come down from this high for a long time. I couldn't wait to see my loved ones. There were parties to attend, I was sure, and I would go to one, but what I was looking forward to the most was tomorrow morning when Tian and I could leave all of this hoopla behind for just a little while. But tonight, we partied!

"HEY, SEXY, WE NEED TO GET UP AND PACK," SOMEONE tall, dark, and incredibly handsome whispered against my shoulder. He dropped a kiss there, then wiggled closer. I moaned, partly in pain, partly in anticipation of a cuddle, and partly because I was too tired, aka hungover, to form words. "How's your head?"

"I've had no complaints," I mumbled as said head began to thump in time with my back bruise, knee bruise, and the bruise on my shoulder from a check into the boards from a certain Canuck last night.

"Ass," Tian chuckled as he nestled in under my arm, the fine hairs on his chest tickling my side. I loved the differences in our bodies. His slim and tight, mine big and... sore. So very sore. "You look like hell. Would you like some OTC stuff?"

I opened my dry mouth to reply when someone hammered on the door. The sounds made my brain ring like a church bell. I was never tossing back shots to celebrate a gold medal ever again. And that was easy to stick to since my craggy ass was just about done being beat like a cheap imported rug. Christ, everything hurt.

"If that's my sister tell her I disowned her," I growled, eyes watering, as Tian leaped from the bed like a gazelle. How? How could he not be suffering? He'd been at my side last night, same as Fiona, rocking shots of tequila until the wee hours at some club. Not sure what the name of the club was. Something Italian. Nice place. I think.

Fiona entered with her usual regal grace. "Christ, you look like shit," she declared, whipping open the room-darkening curtains. My eyes melted. "You have an hour until checkout. I have a ride scheduled to take you to your love nest so rise and shine. Come on." She clapped her hands. Bad words fell out of my mouth. I shoved a pillow into my face. Maybe I would suffocate, and my agony would be over. Someone stronger than me tugged it off then kissed me on the lips.

"Come on, sunshine." Tian eased me into a sitting position while my extremely mean sister started throwing clothes into suitcases. "We have one more round of press to do then we can be alone. All alone. Like just the two of us alone."

Okay, that sounded good. The presser? Not so much. Somehow, I managed to shower. That was it in terms of personal grooming. No shaving or combing of the hair. Just a swipe of deodorant on my pits and a swig of hot coffee that my maybe not-so-mean sister had delivered via room service.

We met the press in the lobby, several dozen hockey players, men and women, and did the blah-blah thing. Yes, we were happy we'd won. Yes, we were anxious to get home. Yes, Milan had been amazing. Yes, we were tickled to get that nice payout for the gold, silver, and bronze medals we had won. There were also sponsorships that would come flowing in for the winners, but I had enough of those. I'd not done this for sponsors like the younger athletes had, I'd done it to prove to myself that I could. And also, to be with Tian.

Our time was short. We needed to figure out where we were going as a couple.

Smiling as politely as a man with a bruised kidney, a swollen knee, and a hangover the size of a Zamboni, I excused myself from the throng. Tian was seated at the bar eating a breakfast burrito, his after-medal media stuff concluded for the moment. My tummy growled at the sight of his platter of food. Fiona was on her phone, talking to someone, probably some horny Italian Olympian that I would have to—

"Excuse me, Jack," someone to my left called in a thick accent. I stopped and turned. The Latvian player who had jacked me in the back stood in front of me, light eyes filled with remorse. "I'd like a moment, please, of your time. I'm Andrejs Briedis. The one who hurt you."

"Yeah, I recall the face but not the name. Your English is good," I tossed out to be polite.

"I want to apologize for your injury. I lost my temper. That is not an excuse to be proud of, but it is the honest one. I did not wish for you to miss games. Have you healed well?"

"Well enough to win the gold."

"Yes, I watched. Wonderful defensive game. I am sorry. Genuinely so."

I felt he was being sincere. Surely he didn't have to linger around and track me down to be insincere.

"Thanks. It's all good. Hockey is a tough game. You

played well." I offered him a hand. He clasped it then shook it heartily. "You're welcome to join us for a quick bite before we check out."

"Sorry, no time. Check out is in ten minutes and the ride is here now. Tian, finish that up. Get your bags and follow me to the exit." Fiona began motioning us along.

"My sister. Very pushy," I explained to Andrejs as Tian jogged past, cheeks puffed out like a chipmunk, a huge carryout bag on his shoulder. "I better go. Nice to meet you."

Fiona steered us to the front desk, out of the door, and into a taxi. "You're on your own now. I have a date in two hours. The driver has the address of the hotel. It's to die for. Enjoy and please romance each other madly." She kissed my cheek then Tian's before shoving us into the back of the taxi.

"Wonder who her date is," I said as we sped away from the Olympic Village.

"Ugh, I never ate a burrito that fast. I think I might die," Tian moaned as we raced, and I do mean raced, through narrow streets my truck back home wouldn't have been able to fit through.

Thankfully, Tian did not die nor did I. If we had we'd have missed out on the suite Fiona had booked for us in a five-star hotel overlooking the Naviglio Grande, a thirty-one mile long canal. I'd never seen such luxury in my life. The room was enormous, with a balcony looking down over the canal. White, brown, and gold bedding and drapes gave the room a classy look. A massive bed, hardwood floors, a huge bath with a rainfall showerhead Tian was already making plans for.

We fell into the bed the moment the porter left our bags by the door. I pulled him close, inhaled the smell of him deep into my lungs, and promptly fell asleep. Sleeping with him by my side under a down duvet until the late morning, showering under a warm rainfall, kissing, touching, making love until the late afternoon then taking a stroll along the canal, hand in hand? Perfect

Typical tourists, we chose to spend the second, and sadly last day, of our mini romantic holiday seeing the sights. We visited the Arch of Peace, ate lunch at a small eatery that made the best saffron risotto, and then made our way to the Cathedral to enjoy the panoramic views at sunset. We were such sightseers it was sickening. I loved every minute. Tian snapped a thousand selfies; most we kept to ourselves even though we were not hiding our relationship. We kissed in public so anyone who cared would know. I heard Tian humming "Adore Me" outside the cathedral and had a flashback to our dance on that pier on the cay. I tugged him into my side to ensure he didn't get away from me again.

Around seven on our final night we found a tiny pizzeria that seated perhaps twenty. We enjoyed an aperitivo of a glass of wine with a dish of large olives, cured meats, cheese, and bread. The waiter allowed us to linger, bringing us more olives and cheese as we listened to a young woman near the door singing Italian love songs. I never wanted to move. Seated here, warm with wine and buzzed from excursions, Tian's hand in mine, watching the people of Milan moving past the open door of the pizzeria...

"This is perfect," I sighed as his dark head came to rest on mine. "Let's never leave."

"I wish we could stay forever too. But you have a hockey game against Philly in two days and I have... well, I have to get back to Colorado and figure out what I'm doing."

I nuzzled my nose into his hair as the street performer began a rendition of "La Cura" that, according to the waiter, had poetic lyrics that added to our romance.

"How will we work this out?" I asked, not moving a muscle when our gorgeous wood-fired Neapolitan pizza topped with cheese, spinach, and prosciutto cotto arrived.

"Let's leave that worry for tomorrow," he replied and so I let it go. He lifted his head from my shoulder, his eyes lazy and heavy lidded, and stole a kiss. "I don't want anything upsetting to slip into this night. I only want us to be happy and desperately in love."

I cupped his cheek. He was warm. "That's easy for me. I'm so crazy in love with you that I don't know up from down."

His mouth found mine again, the kiss slow and searching. If we'd not been in public, I was sure he would have climbed out of his chair to straddle me. Something I would be fully down for back in our suite by the canal.

"I love you too, so damn much. We'll work it out. I promise. Somehow, we'll be together."

Our lips met again. Then once more. I fed him pizza. We laughed. We sang in Italian even though we didn't speak the language. We sipped more wine. We whispered and touched. I fell more in love with him with every glance. If we could sit here for the rest of our lives, listening to the stories of lovers past, eating and drinking, and just being I would want for nothing.

But, we had lives to return to. Lives that were far apart and hidden in the shadows of uncertainty. As they say in Italy if they are roses they will bloom.

Milan sparkled outside the window, the city glowing in celebration. Somewhere out there people were still clinking glasses and shouting in a dozen languages, chasing the high of Olympic history. Inside, in the soft hush of a hotel suite, it was just us.

EIGHTEEN

Tian

JACK WAS SPRAWLED ACROSS THE BED, HAIR DAMP FROM the shower, still faintly flushed from too much kissing. He looked at me as I'd hung the moon, which was ridiculous because I was just a guy who threw himself off ramps with a board strapped to his feet.

"You ever think about what comes next?" he asked me, out of nowhere.

I froze halfway through pulling a T-shirt over my head. "Next?"

"Yeah. After this. After the Olympics, after the season. You and me." His voice cracked a little, as if the question weighed more than the medals on the dresser.

I sat down beside him, brushing my fingers over the Railers hoodie he'd tossed onto a chair earlier, the one I'd stolen more than once. "I try not to. If I think too hard, it feels impossible. You're tied to Harrisburg. I'm always moving. We're..." I trailed off.

Jack's hand slid over mine, squeezing. "We're stubborn enough to make it work."

I stared at him, at the scar along his jaw, at the way his eyes didn't move away. And I thought about that night at the rink when he pressed his hand to the glass and grinned at me as if the world couldn't touch us. I thought about pizza in Milan, grease dripping onto napkins while he teased me about how much I could eat.

And suddenly it didn't feel impossible anymore. It felt inevitable.

The day we left Italy—Jack to Pennsylvania and me to Colorado—was the worst. We'd both been flying high off our medals, and the beautiful time we'd had just the two of us, and splitting apart ripped a hole right through me. Since then, I'd done nothing but miss him, and spent a lot of time at my parents' place, trying to ground myself. I was here again tonight, ready to sit down and watch the Railers game with Dad, who was as big a Railers supporter now as he was NY, something about supporting the man in my life—I loved him for it.

I'd spent the last thirty minutes slumped on the sofa, the scent of food wafting my way, staring at my phone. He'd be getting ready now, only an hour out from the puck dropping, so I decided I wouldn't message him other than the good luck I'd sent him when I'd woken up this morning in my decidedly lonely bed. I must have gone into a deep, dark daze when my cell vibrated because it shocked me so much, I ended up nearly throwing it off my lap.

Jack: *Hey you*

Tian: *Hey you!*

Jack: *Sitting in my cubby, thinking of you*

Tian: *Sitting on Mom and Dad's sofa, thinking of you. Getting dinner, then watching the Railers game.*

Jack: *I'll make it a good one for you.*

Tian: *Big crowd?*

Jack: *Sold out. They're doing a presentation before puck drop, all about the gold medal. I'll be out there feeling stupid but grinning like an idiot.*

God, I wish I could have been there, but I'd had two sponsor meetings today, and two more tomorrow—it seemed everyone wanted a piece of my silver medal-winning ways.

Tian: *I wish I could be there.*

Jack: *I wish you were here. I miss you.*

Tian: *I miss you more. Break a stick for me.*

Jack: *Not happening. But I'll score a goal for you instead.*

I laughed at the screen, cheeks aching from how hard I smiled.

Tian: *I love you, my Jack <3*

Jack: *I love you too, Tian xxx*

I missed him so much it hurt, and sitting at the table

with Mom and Dad, the familiar creak of chairs, the smell of roast chicken—it should have been comfort, but my mind spun circles. I had four more years of chasing medals and points, and with hard work and a lot of luck, going all the way to the 2030 Olympics. But Jack only had a short time on his contract. What then? Would he move to Colorado? Could I ask him to do that? What about Fiona? What about his friends? Was I thinking about long-distance for the next four years? Was that even possible? Should I stop now while I was ahead?

My head hurt.

"I was reading the local paper this morning," Mom said with a little smile. "They called you the pride of the town."

"I saw," Dad said. "And Mrs. Childers at the grocery store taped the clipping right to the counter with a little 'Go Tian!' note underneath."

This should have made me smile, but my thoughts drifted back to Jack, back to what we'd shared and what we hadn't figured out yet. "… and then the elephant walked straight through the produce aisle," Mom finished. "What do you think of that?"

"Hmmm?" I said, not really listening.

"The elephant in the produce aisle," she said.

I blinked, frowning. "Wait, what?"

She arched an eyebrow knowingly. "Exactly. You're not listening."

Heat rushed to my face. "Sorry, Mom."

Dad made a face at me, then picked up the dirty crockery and wandered off to wash up, rattling dishes in the sink. I pushed my chair back to help, but Mom touched my wrist. "Let your father fuss. Sit and talk to me, sweetheart."

I slumped, staring at the table, and for a moment, it felt like being back in school, when Mom was the one who always cut through my tangled thoughts.

"What's wrong, Tian-Lei?"

"Nothing." I scrubbed my eyes. "Everything."

"Is this about Jack?" she asked with her clever-mom perception.

"Yeah," I admitted, my throat tight. "I love him, Mom."

She reached over and grasped my hand. "Of course you do. And he loves you back. It's what we've always wanted for you." Her eyes grew bright with emotion. "It's everything for a parent to see their child happy."

My throat tightened. "I miss him so much. We'd only just gotten together and now we're a million miles apart, and I hate it."

Mom squeezed my hand, then tugged me forward into her arms. I let myself sink into the hug, breathing in the familiar scent of home, wrapped in safety. Mom's hugs were the kind of hugs that made the world stop spinning, that made everything feel solid again, as if nothing bad could reach me while she held me. They were there when I was small, when I'd had problems at school, when I'd realized I was gay, when I'd come out to her and received nothing but unconditional love from her and Dad in return.

"Missing someone means they matter, Tian."

"We're so far apart now."

"That doesn't mean the distance has to win."

I shook my head. "It feels like it is. Some days I don't even know how I'm going to balance it all— training, travel, and him."

"You don't have to have all the answers tonight," she reminded me, her voice steady. "But don't confuse missing him with losing him. Those are two very different things."

Her words sank deep, the kind of wisdom she'd always had when I was a kid and thought the world was too heavy for me to carry.

"I don't know what I'm doing," I admitted. "Snowboarding's everything, but I think Jack is more than that. Should I feel that way?"

"Love is love, Tian."

I groaned. "Love doesn't fix everything, though, Mom. If I keep going, that means years of distance. What if he gives up on me and wants me to quit? And if I walked away…"

Her eyes softened, that quiet strength in them that had steadied me a hundred times before. "Has Jack asked you to stop snowboarding?"

"No." I was horrified. "He wouldn't."

"Is he the kind of man who would ever want you to give up on your dreams?"

"Of course not," I said. The truth of it landed heavy in my chest.

"Then why are you even asking the question?" she asked in her gentle, patient way. "You can love him and still have your career. He'll understand that because the *right* person always does."

"Ready?" Dad asked from the door, tray laden with popcorn and drinks.

Mom caught my gaze. "Love isn't always easy, and long-distance might suck, but it will all work out in the end."

"She's right," Dad added, and made his way to his chair, the same old La-Z-Boy he'd owned forever. Mom always moaned about it sitting there in her otherwise pristine front room, but she never once made him move it. It was like their marriage—full of give and take, of accepting each other, and loving what the other wanted. Watching them, I realized I wanted that kind of love for myself.

I would work for it.

The coverage of the game against Philly started, and I stared at Jack the entire time during warmups. Watching him stretch, bend, fuck, he was pretty—his sandy-ginger hair all tousled, his smile wide and unguarded. When they rolled the Olympic highlights across the Jumbotron, I got so emotional I had to wipe away tears. That was *my* man.

And then they handed him the microphone.

Jack cleared his throat, shifting his weight from one skate to the other, but his voice carried steady across the arena. "Hockey has been my life since I was a kid skating on frozen ponds in Pennsylvania. This medal... it isn't just mine. It belongs to my teammates, to the coaches who believed in me, to the fans who filled every rink with noise and heart, to my family who sacrificed so much. I'm just a piece of something bigger, and I'm humbled to stand here with it."

He paused, scanning the crowd, and I swore for a second his gaze found mine even through the camera. His voice softened. "And there's someone out there who knows exactly how much this means to me. Tian-Lei, you've given me something I didn't even know I needed, and I carried you with me every second on the ice in Italy. This"—he tapped the medal draped around his neck—"is as much yours as it is mine."

The arena roared, but my world narrowed down to him, his words. My chest ached with pride and love so fierce it stole my breath. That was Jack, my Jack, baring his soul to the world and somehow making it feel like it was just the two of us.

"Oh, sweetheart," Mom said and tugged me close. "It will all work out."

As we watched the game, I ran a hundred scenarios

through my head in every break and timeout. Philly and the Railers were evenly matched, every shift a grind, and Jack didn't log as much ice time as usual—probably aching and exhausted from Italy—but even from the bench he never stopped being captain, never stopped barking encouragement and steadying his team. He was beautiful, and he was mine, and I had to figure out a way to make this work.

Could I move closer to him for a year? Harrisburg wasn't the backend of the world. I could rent a place near the rink, train out of a local facility, maybe split my mountain time between Colorado and Vermont. Abel could travel in, or we could do virtual check-ins for conditioning. I could chase the circuit from the East Coast, flying out for comps, still rack up points while being near Jack. The fear came when I thought about what happened after—after his contract ended. Where would we be then? But every time the Railers cleared the puck or Jack leaned into a hit, I told myself I'd deal with later… later. Right now, it was about closing the miles between us.

In the second break, with the Railers and Philly tied at one goal each, I slipped upstairs to my old room. Mom and Dad had kept it pretty much the same— posters still on the wall, the old quilt on the bed—but there was a desk in the corner now where Mom did her crafting, tidy stacks of fabric and half-finished cards spread out. I sat on the edge of the bed and called Abel.

"How would it work if I wanted to move away from Colorado?" I asked.

"What?"

"How would—"

"I heard you," Abel said. "Hang on, I'll take this into the other room." I heard movement, the swish of air, and then a door shutting. "If you're talking Europe, Stubai has one of the biggest training centers—"

"No," I cut him off, heart pounding. "Pennsylvania."

"The what now?"

"Harrisburg to be exact."

There was silence on the other end. "You had all those sponsor meetings, T, shit... Is this you retiring?"

"No. Fuck... no. I don't think so." I rubbed at my face. "Tell me how I can make this work."

"Harrisburg," he pondered. "Home to the Railers and Jack O'Leary?"

"He's my partner," I said, a little defiant in case that was an issue, because it wasn't a fucking issue, and if Abel had a problem with—

"I know that," he said. "I deep-dived when I saw you all moon-eyed over him in Italy, and he has a short time left in his contract—like a year. Do you think he'll stay? Or decide to leave early and move to Colorado."

"He'll stay; I know Jack."

"Agreed, he's one tough son of a bitch." He paused for a moment, and I didn't rush him. "Okay. You could use the facilities at Blue Mountain. It's not Mammoth, but it's workable. You'd need to split your travel time and maintain your conditioning with me virtually. Fly out for major comps, come back to Harrisburg to train in between. It's possible if you stay disciplined."

Possible. The word felt like oxygen. For the first time since leaving Italy, I let myself believe it might work.

"Can you do that?" he asked.

I snapped back to what he said, my head still racing ahead with the image of Jack waiting at the end of every training day.

"Stay disciplined? You know I can." Hell, it was the only thing that had gotten me this far. And if it meant falling into Jack's arms at night, then I'd work twice as hard.

"Some of the sponsors might balk at this."

My stomach tightened, but I forced the words out, sharp with conviction. "Then we'll get my agent to find sponsors who *won't* get pissy at me moving to be closer to the man I love. Simple. I'd rather lose a logo on my board than lose him."

He laughed then, low and knowing, and I felt the first flicker of hope settle deep in my chest.

"You want to do this?" he asked.

"Hell yes."

And as if Jack already knew my plans, he pulled off an ugly-beautiful, standing-on-his-head pass out of the corner, twisting under pressure from two Philly forwards and somehow threading the puck across the slot to Noah Gunnarsson. Gunnarsson snapped it home top-shelf, the crowd exploding, Jack pumping a fist as if the play had been nothing at all.

That was *my* Jack.

NINETEEN

Jack

WAKING UP WITH TIAN IN MY ARMS REMINDED ME OF that old Belinda Carlisle song about Heaven on Earth.

It had taken us some time to get things settled between us. Not the us relationship. That was stronger than ever. The us trying to figure out what we were doing. That had taken some juggling, mostly on his part, which I felt awful about. It seemed as if he had given up a lot for us and I'd not sacrificed a thing. His whole training regime had been upended while I'd done nothing other than buy more towels.

"I can hear you overthinking things," he mumbled sleepily into his pillow. Oh yeah. I had bought a pillow for him too. *Wow, big forfeiture there Jackie Boy.*

"Sorry, I was just lying here admiring the way your back rises and falls when you sleep." I ran a hand over said back, his skin warm and smooth under my palm.

He made a sleepy, yummy sound so I continued to rub his back. "I think I haven't done enough giving in our relationship."

"Jack, no." He flopped to his side to stare at me, the dim morning light tinting the frosty window pink. February into March had been damn cold. Snowy, icy, all the things I usually bitched about, including long nights. Now I enjoyed the long nights. Tian was here now, living out of a hotel for the time being, but here in Harrisburg. "See this is where your ex messed with your head. Sometimes one person gives a lot and the other doesn't. But, no, don't say anything." He placed a toasty finger over my lips. "And then next week or month the other person gives and the other person doesn't. It's not always down to one person to give and the other take. Sometimes you have to carry more of the load, then it's your partner's turn."

I puckered to kiss his fingertip resting on my lips. "Okay, I know that."

"Do you?"

"Yes, I do. I understand. I'm sorry to make it so… mpfhmpfhhfup." He pressed my lips down flat.

"No, no more sorry. I'm happy to make a few changes to make us work. Who knows, maybe when I'm done we'll be looking at moving to Colorado?"

I nodded. Yes, I would gladly do that when I retired. I had one more year with the Railers and that was going to be it for me. My body couldn't take much more. My shoulder was sore from a game against Boston, my knees ached, my back was stiff. My time on the ice was coming to a close, but I still had time to get my team to the Cup finals. I wanted that so badly I could taste it.

"Yeah," I murmured then nipped at his finger. He jerked it back before tossing a muscular leg over my thigh, his flaccid cock nestling into my leg.

"Cool. So now I just need to find a place to live." He sighed as he began to rub the sole of his foot up and down my hairy shin, his hand falling from my lips to lay on my chest. "I mean hotel life is nice, but you know... it's a hotel."

"Why don't you move in with me?" I said, aware of what an enormous bomb I had just dropped on us. His head rose from my pec with such speed he could have whiplashed himself. Dark eyes were round as silver dollars.

"What?"

"Move. In. With. Me." I watched a whirlwind of emotions cross his face. "I mean it's small sure, but we can do two here. And if it's just for another year and a half we can make it work. You already have a towel and a toothbrush..."

"Well, yeah, but a towel and a toothbrush don't mean..." He propped his head up with his hand to stare at me. "You're serious?"

"As a tax collector."

"Wow I just..." His eyes grew dewy. "I would love

that but it's a huge step, Jack. Are you sure you want me and my shit underfoot?"

"I would love to have you and your shit under my feet."

He smiled, a rich, pure smile that made my stomach tighten with love. Then he kissed me, hard and with incredible passion, given we'd fucked each other into the mattress twice last night. My dick was starting to stir when my phone began to chirp.

"Ignore it," Tian whispered over my lips.

I tried, I really did, but the buzzing went on and on. "I'd better check it. Maybe Fiona has had some sort of incident or something."

He sighed but let me move to my side to paw at the nightstand. The bottle of lube we'd used last night fell to the floor with a thud. My fingers skimmed over the vibrating cell. I brought it closer. It was not Fi but Noah Gunnersson.

"It's Gunny," I said over my shoulder. Calling at ten after six? We all woke early as the morning skate started at nine sharp, but a kid his age calling me at the ass crack of dawn meant something serious. "I think I should take it. Sorry. Love you. We'll pick this up after I see what the kid wants."

"Go for it," Tian yawned as he curled into my back like a cat.

"Gunny, what's up?" I asked as I let my head fall

back to my pillow. Tian slung his arm over my hip, his fingers awfully close to my dick.

"It's all over the web," Noah said, his voice strained. The worry in his voice made me tense. What was all over the web? If Trick had done something, stupid I was going to—"Preston Mills is reporting again that a deal with Jari Lankinen is about to hit." Oh man, not this again. That rumor had been cooking on a low heat for months. Yes, we were now one day from the first of March, and the trade deadline was about to roar to life. Things in the league went a little insane around this time of year. Teams looking to bolster their rosters for the upcoming playoffs would be making moves. But bringing a Lankinen to Harrisburg? Surely not. "And Lincoln Reese who writes the Penn Skate blog is also telling people to look for this deal to be done and signed by noon today."

"Okay, Gunny, we've been over this," I said, wishing I'd turned my phone off last night. Not that I didn't love the kid. I did. But he did tend to get a little overly stimulated when it came to his family, rightfully so. And while Tennant Rowe wasn't technically a relative, Noah had grown up with Ten, Jared, and their kids so he was like a beloved uncle to Gunny. "Until we hear it from the team we can't let the trade rumors fuck with our heads."

"But—"

"No, no buts. Look, this is probably just some wild

speculation. I know for a fact that Mills has said some off-the-wall shit to get clicks and calls into his show."

Lincoln Reese on the other hand…

He was one of the most respected sports reporters in this area. And while he mostly focused on the local college teams, he also did a lot of stories on the Railers. So perhaps there was a stink in the air Reese was sniffing at as well. Didn't mean a thing though. Trade rumors were hot commodities for the media. Speculation ran wild online with fans joining in to fan the flames. Ninety-five percent of the whispers were bullshit and never panned out.

"But if he *is* traded to the Railers…"

"If he is, and that's a big if, we'll treat him like any other new player. So, for now, go back to bed with your man and get some sleep. Coach is going to work us hard to make sure we're ready for the Carolina game tomorrow afternoon."

There was a long hesitation on the other end. "Okay, sure, fine. Yeah, you're right. I'm overreacting. No way would the owner allow a trade like that."

"Exactly. Go back to bed. See you at the practice facility and don't be late."

"I won't be. Thanks, Cap."

I chucked my phone to the table, sighed wearily, and felt a stiff dick poking me in the ass.

"Did you turn that off?" Tian asked then started nibbling on my shoulder.

"I did," I purred as he gave me another poke.

"Excellent, pick up the lube. You're going to need it."

Turned out that it wasn't just clickbait and *Ice Beat in the 'Burg* as well as Lincoln Reese had scored a genuine coup. As we were coming off the ice after morning skate Coach called me into his office and closed the door.

"Coach," I asked, feeling a certain cold vibe in the room that had nothing to do with ice. "Problem?"

"We've just given up two future first-round draft picks for Jari Lankinen out in Detroit." His lips were so flat it was a wonder he could force words through them.

"Oh shit," I whispered, dropping into a chair in front of his desk, sweat running down my spine to give me a chill. "That's not going to play well in the locker room. Gunny was already edgy just from the rumors. Why the hell would they bring in someone with such a terrible history with the team?"

"The owner insists that the son should not suffer for the sins of the father," he said as he sat down with a huff. That was true but still... "He's got talent, but he's having trouble settling on any team he's played on, and to be honest, we need his speed on the second line. We'll be moving guys around to accommodate him.

He'll be here tonight and will play tomorrow against Carolina. Tell the team. Inform them that we do *not* want any bullshit over this. What happened to Rowe in the past is just that. In the past. This is now and we need his talent. The first time I hear any shit from anyone, and that includes Noah, I will bench their asses. We are not going to allow this to derail us."

Super. This should be a fun talk. "Okay, Coach, I'll pass that along." I rose, nodded, and exited his office with the weight of a boulder on my shoulders. Pulling up short outside the locker room, I took a hefty breath, walked in, and felt twenty-four sets of eyes on me. "Guys, settle down. I've got some news to pass along."

It was not a fun talk. The mood of the room shifted from upbeat to barely suppressed anger in the space of two minutes after I made the announcement. Ten Rowe and his husband were beloved and admired alumni of this team, so I got the mutters of disapproval from the men. Not only did they have to look at the offspring of someone who had nearly ended a brilliant career, they had to accept line changes because of him. Gunny, amazingly enough, was quiet even when the others were bitching. I'd pull him aside later. For now, I let the initial bad feelings flow before I held up my hands.

"Okay, hey, okay, I get it. That name leaves a bad taste on a lot of tongues in this town. I know Tennant and Jared. I like them both. I like their kids and their charities. I get it. Aarni was a cheap shot artist. Lots of

216 • RJ SCOTT & V.L. LOCEY

old-time players were. Shit, some today are still that way, but as Coach said that was then and this is now. Jari is not his father. He's got talent and he's our new teammate. If you don't like it then talk to the owner, your union rep, or the GM. Coach and me are just the messengers so while we get it and will gladly listen to your complaints, we can't do jack shit about it. So, hit the showers, go home, and bring your game faces to the ice tomorrow morning for skate."

I turned and made for my locker, eager to shower, go home, and work out exactly what the hell I was going to say to Lankinen when he showed his face at the barn tomorrow morning. It was going to be interesting to say the least.

FIDDLING AROUND IN THE SHOWER WAS A GREAT WAY TO avoid the team and the press. The media had leaped onto the Lankinen story like hungry hyenas finding a wounded gazelle. Also, I needed time to think about what to say to Gunny to ease his upset. I knew that his dads, especially Stan, were incredibly close to the Rowe-Madsens. Stan and Ten were like brothers. I also knew that to this day Tennant still suffered headaches from the brain injury brought about by Aarni. This whole situation sucked. What the GM was thinking escaped me.

I lathered my beard as I tried to think of what could have possessed our general manager to make such a trade. Surely the guy had to know this was going to upset the apple cart. It pissed me off a little because our locker room had been a place of camaraderie and high spirits. Now we'd have to tiptoe around Jari Lankinen and Gunny as they worked that shit out, as well as spend valuable time soothing hurt feelings about line changes. And I got it. I really did. Switching players on lines that were gelling like our four was wrong. Especially mid-season when we were rolling along like the steam locomotives on our sweaters. I sucked in a breath and then stuck my face under the hot water. I disliked talking bad about management, but whoever had thought this move up needed their fucking heads examined.

Looking down at my wrinkled hands I knew I had to exit the showers with a towel round my waist and my little shower bag of soap, shampoo, and beard wash. Slippery wet feet squeaks from my Crocs filled the locker room which was now empty. Or mostly so. Gunny was waiting for me, his curls still damp from his shower, his eyes sharp as a hawk. Great.

"You said it was clickbait," he opened with before I even made it to my locker.

"I thought it might be. Hoped it might be," I admitted, opening my locker to expose my street clothes hanging inside. I looked over my shoulder at him sitting in front of his locker, dressed and ready to roll yet still here. With a sigh I turned to face him, water dripping from my beard to trickle down the thick hair on my chest. "Gunny, I am sorry. I assumed no one in their right minds would bring that kid here. He's going to have one hell of a hard time and that sucks for him. You guys being upset sucks for you. This is out of my hands. I wish I could ease the stink of this decision but I'm just a grunt who hits people for a living."

Whatever the future held for us, and my team, it would work out because I had Tian in my life. A man could face any storm with the person he loved beside him.

Epilogue

TIAN

Two months later

AIRPORTS USED TO FEEL LIKE STOPGAPS, AS IF I WAS always halfway between where I'd been and where I was going. But walking through arrivals in Harrisburg and spotting Jack leaning against the wall in his Railers cap, I didn't feel halfway anymore. I felt like I'd come home.

He caught my eye instantly, as he always did, and that grin—God, that grin—cut through the crowd. He pushed away from the wall, weaving through families and suits and a kid dragging a stuffed penguin by its flipper, until he was right in front of me. He cut through the crowd as if I was the only person in the terminal. Which, to me, he was. I was surprised he wasn't surrounded by fans and photographers, given how the

Railers were the favorites for the Stanley Cup this year. The season may well have ended, but the playoffs started in two days, and despite some issues since the Olympics, it was the Railers everyone looked to.

"Welcome home," he murmured, pulling me into his chest.

I laughed into the hug, the scent of cedar detergent and something uniquely Jack hitting me full force. "Thought I was just visiting."

"You're wearing my hoodie. That makes you an official Harrisburg fan."

I glanced down at the worn Railers sweatshirt I'd stolen from his room on my last visit. I hadn't even realized I'd worn it for the flight. Typical.

"Guess I am then."

"Welcome back," he said, pulling me into another hug so solid I nearly forgot the suitcase banging against my shin.

"My Jack," I mumbled into his chest. "Missed you."

"Missed you more." He kissed me right there, in front of families, businessmen, the bored TSA officer pretending not to watch. I kissed him back, because why the hell wouldn't I?

We drove straight to his place, the familiar sprawl of Pennsylvania rolling by the windows. Harrisburg wasn't Colorado. It wasn't the Alps or the X Games or the Olympic Village. It was brick houses and leafy streets, and a hockey arena that still lit up like a beacon on game nights. And it was where Jack lived. That was enough.

Inside his condo—our condo—everything was the same, and the second Jack dropped my bag and tugged me into the living room, it felt warm. Home.

Us.

"Your mom and dad are in the hotel already. I booked us into the same one."

I wish we could have all stayed here, but we didn't have the space, so I had been researching other, bigger, and better options. My career took me all over the country. Jack was here with friends, and my parents were talking about how much they loved the area, suggesting that if I stayed in PA, they might move as well. Then Jack casually mentioned he'd like kids someday and asked if I was interested.

Kids.

Me?

Hell, yes I was. It sounded awesome. Perfect. Everything I wanted with Jack.

So, yeah, we needed a bigger place, and Jack agreed, but that was a discussion for after the playoffs, not before. The same delay applied to the information I compiled on both surrogacy and adoption channels.

We collapsed onto the sofa in a tangle of limbs. His jersey smelled faintly of sweat and cedar detergent, and he had a scrape across his jaw from practice, proof he still threw himself into hockey like it was life or death.

"How long are you here this time?" he asked, brushing a thumb over my cheekbone because he couldn't stop touching me.

"Six weeks," I said. "California, after that, and I found us a place to rent if you want to join me for your summer break."

"Of course I do."

"But between now and then? You're stuck with me here."

His grin softened into something private, almost shy. "Good. I've got plans for us for after the playoffs."

"Plans?"

"Yeah. Stuff normal guys do. Like grocery shopping. Pizza on the couch. Maybe forcing you to sit through every *Rocky* movie in order."

I laughed because he meant it. And maybe that was what I loved most about Jack O'Leary—not the goals, not the medals, not the captaincy. But the way he wanted the same ordinary things I did, the things we'd both been denied by pressure, fame, fear.

"Sounds perfect," I whispered.

We sat there for a while, just existing. The TV played some rerun neither of us watched. My hand fit against his chest, steady and solid, like proof he wasn't going anywhere.

When the pizza was delivered, he handed me a slice, extra cheese, grease already soaking through the napkin. "Authentic Milan flashback," he said with a smirk.

I laughed so hard I nearly dropped it. "Only difference is no paparazzi outside the window."

"Don't jinx it," he warned, but his arm stayed slung around my shoulders, tight, claiming.

"How's the team?" I asked after a yawn, and snuggling deeper into his arms.

"Still hard work," he admitted. "Something's got to give, otherwise we'll fuck up the run to the cup."

"You'll win this year," I said with conviction and he kissed me, slow and certain.

"Hey, Tian?" he murmured.

"Yeah?"

"Love you."

I smiled against his shoulder. "Love you more."

I thought back to Milan, to medals and promises, to the sharp ache of leaving him at the airport. Back then, I'd wondered if we'd make it. Now, sitting here with his arm around me and the future stretching out like a mountain run waiting to be carved, I knew we would.

Because love wasn't just the highs—the medals, the wins, the headlines. Love was this. Pizza boxes on the coffee table. A hockey game on low in the background. His hand wrapped around mine, tethering me to the life we were building together.

I had it all. Right here.

THE END

WANT TO SEE IF TIAN GETS GOLD IN 2030? CLICK HERE for a free bonus short.

Years after their island fling turned into forever, Jack and Tian are husbands, fathers, and still each other's greatest champions. This exclusive bonus scene follows them from quiet moments at home to Tian's triumphant return to the Olympic stage—where love, family, and one breathtaking jump change everything.

https://BookHip.com/SPVQJTT

A legacy he never chose. A love he never expected.

Fly (Railers Legacy 4)

Jari Lankinen never asked to inherit his father's sins, but the name alone is enough to poison every room he walks into. The Railers haven't forgotten the brutal hit Aarni Lankinen delivered to Tennant Rowe, and they sure as hell don't want his son wearing their jersey. Jari is a gifted young forward, flashy and media savvy, with the skill to change games, but his last name makes him a target before he even skates his first shift. Earning respect means pushing through hostility and suspicion, fighting every day to prove he isn't his father. To the fans, he's the son of a villain. To his teammates, he's a reminder of the past. To himself, he's a man trapped in a shadow he can't escape.

A steady force in the high-pressure world of professional baseball, Cameron Blackburn has built his career on focus, discipline, and keeping his head when others lose theirs. He isn't flashy, but he's respected, trusted, and known for bringing balance to every team he's played on. When their paths cross at a shared training facility, Cam is drawn to Jari's restless energy —the fight in every move, the loneliness in his silence, the way he carries his past like armor. Where others feel only wariness at Jari's name, Cam sees someone worth knowing, worth trusting, worth holding onto. And while opening his heart to Jari may test the limits of his own control, Cam has never been afraid to stand firm when the storm comes.

Fly is a legacy, redemption, and opposites-attract romance set against the backdrop of professional sports. Featuring a hockey forward fighting to escape his father's shadow, a disciplined baseball player who refuses to be shaken, the clash of storm and calm, and a love that proves sometimes the biggest risks are the ones worth taking.

Hockey Series' from RJ Scott & V.L. Locey

Harrisburg Railers

Owatonna U Hockey

Arizona Raptors

Boston Rebels

LA Storm

Chesterford Coyotes - Young Adult

Railers Legacy

Rochester Copperheads (AHL, coming soon)

Oxford Knights (coming 2027)

Harrisburg Railers

When hockey wunderkind Tennant Rowe meets his new coach, he knows he's in trouble. Jared Madsen is nine years older than Tennant, impossibly attractive, and — worst of all — his brother's off-limits best friend. Is their chemistry worth the risk?

Changing Lines (Railers 1)

Can Tennant show Jared that age is just a number, and that love is all that matters?

The Rowe Brothers are famous hockey hotshots, but as the

youngest of the trio, Tennant has always had to play against his brothers' reputations. To get out of their shadows, and against their advice, he accepts a trade to the Harrisburg Railers, where he runs into Jared Madsen. Mads is an old family friend and his brother's one-time teammate. Mads is Tennant's new coach. And Mads is the sexiest thing he's ever laid eyes on.

Jared Madsen's hockey career was cut short by a fault in his heart, but coaching keeps him close to the game. When Ten is traded to the team, his carefully organized world is thrown into chaos. Nine years his junior and his best friend's brother, he knows Ten is strictly off-limits, but as soon as he sees Ten's moves, on and off the ice, he knows that his heart could get him into trouble again.

––––––––––

Harrisburg Railers (Hockey Romance)

1. Changing Lines
2. First Season
3. Deep Edge
4. Poke Check
5. Last Defense
6. Goal Line
7. Neutral Zone
8. Hat Trick
9. Save The Date
10. Baby Makes Three

Railers Volume 1 | Railers Volume 2 | Railers Volume 3 | Railers Volume 4

Meet the men of Owatonna University's hockey team

Ryker (Owatonna U, 1)

Ryker is hockey royalty, Jacob is a poor country boy. Can two vastly different people find common ground and become the men they want to be?

Ryker comes from a long line of championship-winning hockey players. Playing college hockey to develop his game is his only focus, and nothing will stand in the way of him working to become the best player. He has no room for relationships, people who point out his flaws, or anyone who calls him on his dreams. He certainly has no place for love, and meeting Jacob is nothing but a useful distraction on the side. After all trying to get his Owatonna Eagles teammate into bed is less work and more play. When tragedy rocks his family, his charmed life crumbles, and the only person he can turn to is the same one who claims to hate him.

Jacob Benson has only known hard work and stifling conservative values his whole life. Born and raised in the small rural community of Eden Crossing, Minnesota, he's the only son of a hard-working but struggling dairy farming family. Jacob is using his skills in hockey to finance his way to an agricultural science degree. These four years at Owatonna U. will probably be the only time he has to enjoy life, gain acceptance about his sexuality, and live openly before his inevitable return to the farm. Running into a pretty rich boy like Ryker Madsen is putting a damper on his enjoyment of life away from home. Ryker's flip, conceited, carefree attitude grates on Jacob's every nerve. So why, if Ryker is everything he dislikes, does he want nothing more than to explore the sinful dreams that his annoying teammate stars in every night?

Ryker

Owatonna U Hockey (Hockey Romance)

1. Ryker

Arizona Raptors

Coast to Coast (Arizona Raptors 1)

Coast To Coast

**When opposites attract, this bottom-of-the-league team
will never be the same again.**

A stipulation in his father's will forces Mark back into the
arms of a family that disowned him and leaves him one-third
owner of a hockey team facing financial ruin. He doesn't even
watch hockey, let alone like it, and wants nothing more than to
head back to New York. Then there's the new coach, a

stubborn, opinionated, irritating man with superiority issues and questionable music taste. Butting heads with Rowen becomes the new normal, but it comes with passionate debate and an all-consuming lust.

Challenged to rebuild one of the worst teams in the league into a future cup contender, Rowen can't pass up the opportunity. Never in his twenty years of hockey has he ever seen a team managed so badly or coached players overflowing with resentment and bigotry. Yet there's something about this team and this city that compels him to roll up his sleeves and start dismantling. If only Mark, one of three siblings who now own the Raptors, wasn't so damned rock-headed yet so damned appealing his job might be easier. It doesn't look like either is willing to give in, but one night in a dark, desert hotel changes everything.

Coast To Coast

Arizona Raptors (Hockey Romance)

Boston Rebels

Top Shelf (Boston Rebels 1)

Acting on the attraction to his best friend's brother has always
been off the table for Xander until a passionate hookup with
Mason at a beach resort begins a love affair that burns long
after summer ends.

Mason specializes in assisting same-sex couples on their
journey to becoming parents and fighting every rule that
blocks his way in the stuck-in-the-past agency that hired him.
Living in his brother's pool house is rent-free, and every cent
he earns he saves for his dream—that one day he'd have his

own company helping others. The downside is that he has to see his annoying brother every day, the upside is that his brother's teammates from the Boston Rebels make regular visits. The eye candy that passes Mason's window is almost enough to make him consider dating a hockey player, but not just any player though. Ever since Xander—his brother's childhood friend—came out as gay at a press conference, Mason's puppy love has turned into a burning attraction he can no longer ignore.

Hockey has been one of Xander's main focuses since he was old enough to balance on skates. Well, hockey and Mason Kingsley, but Mason was always unattainable. Now that he's about to see thirty candles on his birthday cake and is no longer hiding the fact he's gay, he's ready to find a soul mate to make his life complete. A summer vacation is just what he needs to have time to think, but when the Boston Rebels arriving in paradise with Mason in tow, thinking is the last thing he needs. One torrid night under a balmy moon and rules about not messing with his best friend's brother vanish on a warm, tropical breeze.

Summer romances don't generally last past Labor Day, but with the new season about to begin Xander and Mason are going to have to face the world and decide if their love is real enough to withstand everything.

Boston Rebels

Lost In Boston (Free Prequel Novella)

1. Top Shelf
2. Back Check
3. Snowed
4. Royal Lines
5. Blade
6. Rental

LA Storm

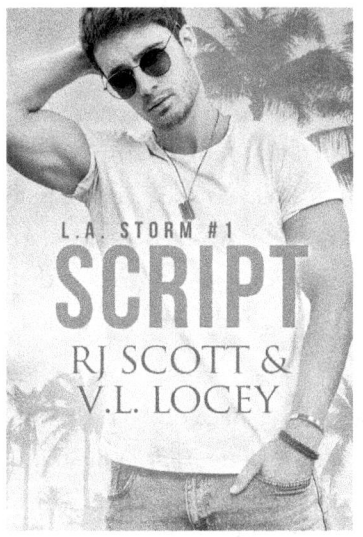

Script (LA Storm, 1)

Script

Hollywood A-lister Finn might be Canadian, but he needs Cameron to show him how to hockey.

Actor Finn Kerrigan is at a crossroads. After growing up a soap star, then starring in a hugely successful trilogy of action movies, he's finally given the chance to read a heartfelt and passionate script that could change his life forever. The role would be enough for people to see him as a serious actor, and maybe even win him an award or two (and no, a golden raspberry award for his action movies doesn't count). Once established as a serious actor he's sure he can come out of the closet and finally live his truth. When he lies to get the part of a hockey player on a struggling team, he suddenly has nowhere to hide. He might be Canadian, but the last time he skated he was ten, and no, he doesn't have hockey in his blood. With only a month until filming starts, he about to be exposed, but partnered with a player who's supposed to be giving him tips, he doesn't realize how many of his secrets will come to light. Falling in lust, one heated kiss at a time, is inevitable, but giving Cameron up at the end of the shoot could break his heart.

Cameron Chavkin is the face of the LA Storm. And the body, and the hair, and the smile. He's at the prime of his career, men and women want to be with him, and he's skating better than he ever has before. His house sits next to a famous rock star's mansion, his garage is filled with expensive cars, and he's even been asked to mentor a once-famous actor in a new hockey movie. Life is pretty sweet. Until the bad boy of hockey meets Finn, a man on the edge with more secrets than Cameron has endorsements. Knowing better than to get involved, Cameron is swept up despite himself, and when it's time to say goodbye to the Storm's most eligible bachelor is finding it hard to follow the script.

Script

LA Storm

1. Script
2. Second
3. Shield
4. Spiral

Speed (Railers Legacy 1)

Hard ice. Fast cars. Fierce love.

And a race against fate.

Hockey is as natural as breathing for Noah. Growing up with two famous hockey stars as his dads, Noah has always aspired to join the Railers to continue the Lyamin-Gunnarsson legacy. With his degree done, it's time to live that dream, and the first step is being drafted by the team his hall-of-fame dad played for. The second step is to pull on that dusky blue-gray sweater and make his fathers proud. His rookie year is bound to be a season of incredible highs and lows, but one of the biggest highlights is meeting Brody Vance at a fundraiser. Brody is the living epitome of a bad boy hiding his pain behind a devil-may-care attitude. As Noah struggles to keep one eye on the puck and not on Brody, it's only a matter of time before both loves collide in a chaotic splash of media attention.

Bad boy racing driver Brody has spent his life chasing speed and glory and is only points away from his first world championship when a devastating crash ends his season. Determined to make a triumphant comeback, Brody is blindsided by a diagnosis that forces him off the track for good. With his world flipped upside down and family and fans questioning why he left, Brody hides his pain by pushing the limits and refusing to let anyone see the cracks. But after a chance meeting with a sweet, sexy hockey player turns into an unforgettable one-night stand, fate keeps putting Noah in his path. With his heart on the line and his body racing against time, Brody must decide if he's willing to risk it all for love—or if he'll let fear and pride leave him in the dust.

Speed is a steamy M/M romance with a hockey rookie living his family legacy, a bad-boy racing driver with secrets, media attention that would break even the strongest of men, an unforgettable one-night stand, a love that means risking it all, and a hard-won happily ever after.

Railers Legacy

1. *Speed*
2. *Blitz*
3. *Powder*
4. *Fly*

Off The Ice (Chesterford Coyotes, 1)

Off The Ice

**A coming-of-age love story with high school, hockey
rivalry, friendship, family, and coming out.**

Soren's life changes in an instant when he and his younger
brother are adopted by hockey royalty. Making sense of his
new life is hard enough, but when he's enrolled in a private
school it means facing a whole new set of problems.
Navigating friendship, family, and hockey is one thing, but

being attracted to the boy who vexes him is a whole new thing.

Felix has a reputation to protect. He's the kid who seems to have everything but looks can be deceiving. Spinning lies about his perfect life, he's created a fantasy world that even he has started to believe. Only, it's not long before everything crumbles, all of his pretty lies are revealed, and only his closest rival sees through his pain and stands by him.

Fighting is easy, friendship is hard, but love is everything.

Off The Ice

Chesterford Coyotes

1. Off The Ice
2. On Thin Ice
3. *Dance on Ice*

Free Reads

Please note - in all of these free stories, there will be some spoilers for the main series books.

Railers Short Stories

Volume 1 | Volume 2

LA Storm

Sparkle

The Colts - AHL Short Stories

Pucks & Percentages

Breakaway

Making the Save

Standalone

Waiting for Christmas

Meet RJ Scott

RJ writes MM romance—sometimes sweet, sometimes dark, always with a generous splash of angst and a hint of hurt/comfort.

A born romantic, she's convinced love is love—and every man deserves his happily ever after (especially the ones who swear they don't).

Website - gayromance.co.uk
Newsletter - gayromance.co.uk/mailing-list

Scan for a complete list of ebooks and links.

instagram.com/rjscott_author
amazon.com/author/rj-scott
bookbub.com/authors/rj-scott

Meet V.L. Locey

V.L. Locey loves worn jeans, yoga, belly laughs, walking, reading and writing lusty tales, Greek mythology, the New York Rangers, comic books, and coffee. (Not necessarily in that order.)

She shares her life with her husband, her daughter, one dog, two cats, a flock of assorted domestic fowl, and two Jersey steers.

When not writing spicy romances, she enjoys spending her day with her menagerie in the rolling hills of Pennsylvania with a cup of fresh java in hand.

vllocey.com | vicki@vllocey.com
Newsletter - vllocey.com/newsletter

Scan for a complete list of ebooks and links.

facebook.com/V.L.Locey

x.com/vllocey

instagram.com/vl_locey

bookbub.com/authors/v-l-locey

goodreads.com/vllocey

pinterest.com/vllocey